THE SIBYL

THE SIBYL

PÄR LAGERKVIST

TRANSLATED BY *Naomi Walford*

VINTAGE BOOKS
A Division of Random House
New York

THE SIBYL

IN A LITTLE HOUSE on the mountain slopes above Delphi lived an old woman with her witless son. The house consisted of a single room; one wall was the mountain side itself, and always dripped with moisture. It was really not a house at all, but a ramshackle hut which herdsmen had built for themselves. It stood quite alone away up in the wild mountain, high above the buildings of the city and above the sacred precincts of the temple. The woman seldom left the house, her son never. He sat within, in the half-light, smiling to himself as he had always done; he was now well into middle age and his lank hair had begun to turn gray. But his face was untouched; it was as it had always been, without any real features in its heardless, downy childishness, only that queer, perpetual smile. The old woman's face was furrowed and austere, and swarthy, as if it had been touched by fire; her eyes had the look of eyes that have seen god.

They lived quite by themselves; no one visited them or had anything whatever to do with them. Two goats gave them milk, and the woman gathered herbs and roots up in the mountain; and that was what they had to live on. They could never have got anything from other people, for no one would have any dealings with them.

The entrance to the house faced the valley, and she often sat in that dim opening, looking down upon the world that she had left so long ago. Nothing was hidden, all lay spread out below her: the city with its people coming and going among their houses, each engrossed in his own affairs; the sacred way along which the pilgrims paced solemnly up to the temple court; the sacrifices offered at the altar before the god's house. All was well-known to her. And sometimes in the morning, early in the morning, a certain thing happened down there which she knew best of all. The court was still empty then; only a youth would be sweeping the ground before the entrance to the temple and strewing fresh laurels from the god's grove. The sun had just risen above the mountains in the east and the whole valley was filled with new light. And a young woman attended by two priests came slowly walking up the sacred way; she had bathed in the spring that welled forth from the cleft in the rock; her face was reverent and her gaze was lifted toward the holy place which she was approaching. She was dressed as a bride, as god's bride. The youth at the entrance to the temple came toward her bearing a bowl of holy water, with which he sprinkled her; and, purified, she stepped into the god's dwelling place to be filled with his mighty spirit. It happened now, and thus it had happened from immemorial times. The old woman sat outside her house and watched it with her old eyes.

Behind her, inside in the half-light, sat her grizzled son, a smile on his downy, childish face.

ONE EVENING before sunset a man came walking up the path from Delphi. There was nothing strange in this; people came that way sometimes to see to their animals at pasture on the mountain. The track passed a stone's throw or so below her house. But this time something happened which surprised her greatly. The man turned off the path and began climbing the steep slope where there was no track at all. Such a thing was unknown; no one had ever left the path to come up here. Who would want to? The slope was covered with loose stones from landslides, and at times he found it difficult to advance. Perhaps he was unused to this country. From her nest she followed him with her old eyes.

He came nearer and she was able to make out his face. She did not know him. But she knew no one— no one now living. He was quite a tall man with a strong, brownish beard, untrimmed and not in the fashion of this country. His cheeks were pale, quite without color, though he had to exert himself greatly to climb the hill. He was a man in the prime of life, perhaps in early middle age.

When he came up to her he made his salutation, but not in the manner of these parts. And when having sat down on the stone bench before the house he began speaking, slowly and at first with some difficulty in finding words, she noted at once that he was a foreigner, and probably from very far away. This could be seen also in his look, which was heavy and old, though he himself was young. But that might be his own look and not that of his race.

He told her that he had come to Delphi to consult the oracle about something of great importance to him. But he had been turned away before he could do so; they would not let him enter the room where the seekers were assembling.

There was no answer to what he asked, they told him. No oracle in the world could answer it.

Dejectedly he left the temple court, and wandered at random about the city all that day. More than once he thought of leaving Delphi, where he had nothing to hope for, and of going further—somewhere—anywhere. Then, in a dirty alley in the poorest quarter of the town, he had got into conversation with an old blind man, a very old beggar who crouched at a street corner and held out his shaking hand in the hope that someone would drop something into it. This seemed an odd thing in a street where all must have been equally poor, but he said that in earlier days he had begged in the temple court and beside the sacred way, though now he could no longer go so far. "When we had begun to talk of this together I told him of my own cares, of my long, vain wayfaring to Delphi, and of my distress because the oracle had been unable to give me an answer. He listened to me with compassion and understood me well, though he thought it strange that there should be anything which the Delphic oracle could not answer. 'You must have put hard questions,' he said.

"But when he had thought it over he went on reflectively: 'There may be one who can help you. One who can answer all that a man can ask.' And he told me that up in the mountains there lived an old priestess of the oracle, an ancient pythia, cursed and hated by all because she had committed a crime against god. Against the temple and against god and against all sacred things; yet she was a great and mighty sibyl. No priestess in Delphi had ever been so great, so beloved and possessed by god as she. She had prophesied with her mouth wide open, and no one had been able to endure the sight of her when she was filled with her god. His own breath had issued from her mouth and her speech had been as wild as fiery flames, it was said; for thus did he love her. He refused to speak through anyone but her, and did so for many years.

"But then she had sinned against both god and man and cast herself down into damnation; she had been driven from the city with sticks and stones and had been cursed by all men and of course by the god —by him whom she had offended. 'This happened in my childhood,' said the old man, 'but although no one speaks of her any more or utters her name, she is said to be living still, in the mountains whither she was driven. And I don't doubt that it is true. One who has been in such contact with the divine must find it hard to die, with such power as must yet remain within her. One in whom god has once taken up his abode he does not forsake, though he remain only as a curse.

" 'Seek her out, and you'll surely get an answer to your questions, though it may appall you.'

"And he pointed with his trembling hand to this mountain, and blind though he was he pointed aright."

She to whom he had been speaking sat motionless, as she had sat throughout his tale. No change in her face revealed what might be stirring within her. Searchingly and with some surprise he gazed into the dark, furrowed face, as if to read in that old book which, for all its plain script, was so difficult to decipher. It was as if it had been written in an ancient tongue which was no longer spoken.

For a long time she sat silent, seemingly abstracted, withdrawn into herself.

"What was it that you asked the oracle?" she said at last, as if she had wakened from her musing.

"I asked about my destiny," he said.

"Your destiny?"

"Aye, my destiny. My life—how it's to be. What awaits me."

"That's what most people ask; that's all they're curious about. What is so extraordinary in your destiny? Is it something special?"

"Yes, it is."

And he told her of a peculiar thing that had happened; an event which had scored itself so deeply into his memory that he seemed not to recall anything besides; an event which left his soul no peace, which had impelled him to come to Delphi and now at last to her, to seek enlightenment and some measure of peace.

I lived happily with my young wife and my little son, he began, in the city where I was born, and I had no thought of leaving. I had my livelihood there and a house left me by my father. I was not rich, but well-to-do; my life was secure and carefree, and all things seemed to prosper with me.

One day as I was standing at my door I saw an unknown man dragging himself along with his cross. There was nothing extraordinary in this, nothing unusual; it often happened that men who were to be crucified were led along our street by soldiers, up to the gallows place; ours was the road to it. And there was nothing peculiar about the man himself, so far as I could see. He was pale and tired; he seemed exhausted. Because of that, no doubt, he paused and leaned against the wall of my house a little way from where I was standing. I didn't like it. What's he doing that for? I thought. If a condemned man, a man so unhappy, leans against my house, he may bring ill fortune upon it. So I told him to move on, and said I didn't want him there.

Then he turned toward me and when I saw his face I knew that this was no ordinary man—that there must be something special about him. But what it was that made me think so I could not have said. I believe that the look on his face was not usually angry at all, but gentle and submissive. But it was not so now; it was mighty and terrible in a way that I shall never forget.

"Because I may not lean my head against your house your soul shall be unblessed forever," he said.

I was astonished and uneasy, and thought it somehow sinister. The soldiers simply laughed and drove him forward, for they did not want him to stand there either; they forced him on. But before he went further with his cross he turned to me again and said menacingly, "Because you denied me this, you shall suffer greater punishment than mine: you shall never die. You shall wander through this world to all eternity, and find no rest."

And he settled his cross upon his shoulder again and dragged himself on along the street until he disappeared through the gate of the city some way off.

I stayed where I was, with a most strange sensation. Something seemed to have happened to me— something whose inward meaning escaped me. I could not explain it, either to myself or to anyone else, but so it was. Some neighbors who had heard what the man said and saw me standing there and looking queer told me not to trouble myself about it—not to take any notice of what a man like that said: a criminal who was going to be crucified. Surely I knew that they often burst out into the most terrible threats and curses because they were in a rage with everything and because they were to lose their lives. They talk all sorts of rubbish, you know that— it's nothing to vex yourself about.

I knew well enough that they were right. And in taking it as they did—in laughing at me a little and shrugging their shoulders at the incident—they reassured me. When we had chatted about it a little I was laughing at it too; I went back to my work and thought no more about it.

But I couldn't quite forget. It came into my mind now and then, though I tried to drive it out. The day passed, I attended to my work and everything was as usual. Or so I thought. But the words he had spoken remained with me; from time to time they were repeated in my innermost self—by whom? By me? I don't know, but I heard them—I heard them quite plainly. I couldn't understand why I had to recall them; I knew they meant nothing—nothing at all—that they were just words spoken to me by an unknown criminal because he had not been allowed to lean his head against my house. There was no more to it than that, and it was foolish to pay any attention to what he'd said. Why did I do it?

I thought that by next day I should have shaken it off. But when I woke in the morning it was with the sense of something having happened to me, and as I lay dozing, the same words were slowly repeated inside me, and softly—as it were in a whisper— they reminded me of the sentence that had been passed on me—by whom?

When I had risen I was myself again, and I set about my work as usual. But I felt no real inclination for it—I, who was usually so eager and took such pleasure in it. After a time I became too restless to sit still, and I wandered about idly doing nothing at all. I had no wish to do anything. This was quite un-like my usual self. And so it went on, day after day. In some way I had altered and could not recognize myself.

I don't know how long it was before I heard the queer rumor that the man who had been taken along our street to be crucified was god's son. It was not said openly, but whispered among people in the city and talked about in secret. Those who really ought to have known the truth of it—those who believed in him—seemed to be in hiding and dared not come forth to bear witness on his behalf—not yet. There cannot have been many of them; most people in the city didn't believe it at all, of course; they thought it was some foolish invention, and those who had had him executed declared it to be a blasphemy against god.

God's son—of course he wasn't, I told myself. It's ridiculous. Quite absurd. God's son? . . . And I asked about this rumor, about how it had begun and who were spreading it; naturally it was those who believed, those who were in hiding. They declared that a miracle had come to pass—all kinds of miracles—showing that it was true; and then the miracle of their own belief: that they knew him to be the son of god and had experienced it in themselves. For them, this was of course the greatest, most important miracle. They were not at all reliable people, and what they said was unworthy of attention.

I discussed it with the neighbors, asking them their opinion; asking what they thought of the story that the criminal—if they remembered him—who had dragged himself past with his cross was god's son. They had heard of it, too, and thought it arrant nonsense.

But many believe it, I said. They shrugged their shoulders and said something about lunatics.

"Are you still brooding over what he said to you?" one of them added with a laugh.

"Not in the least," I answered, laughing too. "Are you mad? You don't think I'd care about a thing like that?"

But was that true? Did I really not care about it? It was easy enough to say; but why then did I feel so changed, so downcast and joyless, and why did everything seem so meaningless? Why had it become so? Why did everything seem so empty and desolate somehow, both within and around me? I had never felt thus before. What sort of change was it? Why did I feel like this?

I remember one day I was walking outside the city gate in the fertile countryside I knew so well: the vineyards and the fields of grain, with olives and fig trees in them. I marveled to see how drab and depressing it all looked, for as a rule it was quite the opposite. It was the middle of the day, but it felt more like evening, and I was oddly oppressed by the sight of that landscape and its gray desolation. What did it mean? What was the matter with me?

Was this my world? The world I was to live in?

And I remember with how heavy a tread I turned back to the city and my home.

As yet I had said nothing to my wife; I had not wanted to. But she must have noticed it. Mustn't she? So I went into the room where she usually was at that time of day to tell her about it, and what it was like.

I found her lying on a straw mat on the floor, playing with her child; I broke in upon their game. I explained to her as best I could what was the matter with me, and that I believed I had been laid under a curse.

She laughed at me as she lay there on her back

playing with the baby and holding it high in the air; he had such a young and lovely laugh.

"Yes, I think you must have been," she said, "seeing how long it is since you kissed me."

I tried to smile and stood watching them, knowing that this was something beautiful and something that I dearly loved; yet a sort of gray ash seemed to lie upon them, as it lay upon all I saw.

And I felt like a stranger standing there, like some outsider who ought not to disturb them in their life. When I went away I heard them go on with their play.

As they were, so had I been but lately—delighting in life, in being alive; I had rejoiced in it every day.

Every day? . . . It was strange; he had said that I should live forever—that I should never die. How strange . . . Why should I mind that? Had it not always been my dearest wish never to have to die, never to die? Why then did I not rejoice? Why did I feel no gladness?

. . . "to all eternity, and find no rest."

I had never really thought about it before, but now I seemed to gain some inkling of what eternity was. That it would deprive me of my life. That it was itself the damnation, the unblessedness; that it would itself unhallow my soul.

Eternity . . . It has nothing to do with life, I thought; it is the contrary to all life. It is something limitless, endless, a realm of death which the living must look into with horror. Was it here that I was to dwell? Was it for that that this thing had been given me? "To all eternity . . ." That was my death sentence: the most cruel that could be devised.

This god takes from me all the joy of living, I whispered to myself.

For the first time I glimpsed the existence that awaited me, and looked into its void. And for the first time I truly believed in the power of this curse —I believed that this questionable god could carry out his intention and that my soul would become just as he had threatened; that all would be accomplished as he had said.

Yes, all was being accomplished. The change in me went forward and I was helpless to arrest it. What power had I? What was I to do? How could I act, how prevent what was happening? I had no power, I was utterly impotent. For I was myself the unhallowed soul I desired to help, I was myself the transformation that was taking place within me and filling me with perdition.

One day in my despair I did something—something that was only to increase my unhappiness, my unblessedness. It was the middle of the day, but I lay outstretched upon my bed, tormented by my hurrying thoughts, by my inner self, my own inner self—the thing that was no longer mine. Suddenly I was seized with fury at my destiny and the malignant god to whom I owed it. Why should I accept it? This madness? Why did I not rebel against the power within me and say: I will not! I will not! I will live, I will live exactly as others live and be as I have been. I will be like everyone else! I will live!

And when I had said this—I said it aloud, though to myself—it was as if the curse fell from me like a heavy garment; I felt a relief, a liberation such as I had never known before during all the time that had passed. And I rose and went into the room in which my wife and the child were. For a while I stood watching their prattling play; then I went up and gently separated her from the child and kissed her. She put her arms about me and they were bare and warm, and we went into my room together, and when we had undressed she lay down on my bed with the little smile I knew so well—on the bed where but now I had lain in torment—and parted her knees for me to come at her. All was as before when we had loved each other, and I thought I had conquered, and regained my happiness.

But I could do nothing. I felt how ravishing she was, more ravishing than ever—I knew that—because it had been so long; yet I was not filled with any desire. Her warmth flooded to meet me, but it was she alone who was warm; I grew cold and damp and could do nothing. Her breath panted against my face, panted for me. But I was powerless.

At last I burst out weeping—I lay despairing on her glorious warm body and wept.

She stroked my hair a little, and my cheek. Then she took my head between her hands and looked at me, looked closely, searchingly at me, into my face, as she had not done for a long time.

"How old your eyes have grown," she said.

Now my unhappiness was complete; it was like a bottomless well into which I had been hurled, now that this too had been taken from me. But was it so strange? It was life's greatest bliss. Was it strange that it should be taken from me, that I should not know it—never know it again? I the unblessed? I, condemned to eternal unblessedness?

After this, others too began to notice the change in me, or so at least I fancied. People avoided me, withdrew from me, I thought; and if they were compelled to speak to me and meet my eyes they looked at me queerly. The neighbors in our street fell silent, and seemed to realize at last that something had happened to me and that it had to do with the man who was taken out to be crucified and whom I forbade to lean his head against my house. They never spoke to me about it, and as I say they avoided me; yet it was clear that they had noticed the alteration in me— that they observed me secretly and whispered about me, and that it was from compassion alone that they refrained from saying: How old your eyes have grown.

My wife became more and more shy of me; something in me seemed to frighten her—no doubt my eyes. And she must have remembered my telling her that a curse had been laid upon me. I don't know, for we never talked of it, and what had happened between us we never hinted at by so much as a word.

She doesn't want to look into them any more, I told myself.

No doubt she suffered as keenly as I did from the change I had undergone. I don't know, for we never confided in each other; neither of us knew what burden of thought the other bore. And after the time I've spoken of, our eyes never met again.

I had never concerned myself about her thoughts, in any case. She was like a child, and I had never gained much by talking to her, though this had not struck me before and I had been content with her childish prattling. Now I understood the futility of talking to her about anything, and I did so no longer. Her mere presence began to exasperate me, and the knowledge that she was somewhere near— even the sound of her voice or her laughter somewhere about the house. But she didn't laugh so often now. For the most part she stayed with the child; I suppose they still played together in there, but more quietly than before; they could hardly be heard. Thus everything in the house was greatly changed.

I was bound to bear rancor against her because I had been unable to go into her; I had to take revenge upon her for that. I did so now. I never looked at her, neither at her nor at the child, but behaved as if they weren't there. I had never been particularly attached to my son, in any case—or had I? At least I had always thought that she fussed over him too much, no doubt because she was a child herself; and the secret grudge I had borne against him broke out now that I was cut off from her forever. What troubled her more than anything, I knew, was that what had happened was being visited on the child; and more and more often it could be seen that she had been crying. For although I avoided looking at her I always noticed that.

Unhappiness does not make a man good. If I suffer, why should not another suffer?

Yet I never said anything directly unkind to her; she could not reproach me for that. I said hardly anything at all, and never allowed my resentment to find expression; I kept it entirely to myself. All the same, she must have felt what was going on in me. Malevolence, like love, needs few words.

The whole house became desolate, silent and joyless; my wife crept about sorrowfully and my child hid from me when I came near.

I was none the happier for this. Although it was by my own wish, my soul grew the sadder for it, the more unblessed. I would often stand staring in front of me, or out of the window, with empty eyes, seeing nothing and without really knowing that I was there; like a prisoner locked up in himself. Or I wandered restlessly through the gray countryside outside the city gates, where trees and fields were covered with ashes. And so it went on for I know not how long.

One day she was gone. She and the child. To my own surprise I rushed all over the house looking for them, and when once again—after I cannot say how many times—I burst into the room where they had always played together and from which one could always hear their laughter (though not lately)—when I went in there again and realized at last that they were not there and never would be there again, I sank down with a shriek. For it was as if a knife had been driven into my breast and I lay bleeding, on that little mat of straw where once she had lain on her back and lifted up her child with her bare arms. How long I lay there I cannot tell. But then I heard something, more and more distinctly; a voice inside me, and I had to sit up. I sat staring before me. Over and over again, louder and louder I heard it—heard what he had said—the frightful words that he had pronounced over me. My inner self was full of them, echoed with them; it was as empty as a deserted house, and between the bare walls there reverberated eerily those menacing words about my destiny—about what lay before me. His curse resounded through my soul.

That same evening, unknown to any, I left the city of my birth and walked out into the darkness, to begin my wandering through the ages. In the loneliness of night I took the first steps along the road of my malediction.

Since then I have roamed without a halt; without rest, as I am bound to do and, like him, finding nowhere to lay my head. I have wandered about a world covered with ashes, with a layer of gray ashes: the world that is mine. I have seen in it all human wretchedness, all want and evil. I have learned that it is like me, as evil and loveless as I who am to live in it forever; that this is my world, the world of the homeless, god-accursed man with a soul forever unblessed.

From time to time I have come upon those who believe in the man who condemned me to this life. It has happened more and more often, for it seems that his teaching has spread far and wide. These people seem happy, whether from simple-mindedness or some other cause—perhaps because of their faith; that is what they say themselves, of course. And it may be true. To them he seems to have brought blessing, that same god who to me has brought so great a curse. And they say he is good and loving—aye, that he is love itself for the man who believes in him and devotes himself to him. It may be so. It does not concern me. For me he is a malignant power which never releases me from its talons, and gives me no peace.

That he really is god—that the man who was led along our street past my house to be crucified really was god's son—they do not doubt. They have so many signs of it, they say: that he rose from the dead and ascended into heaven, carried up in a cloud—and many, many other things. But none of that concerns me. Their faith, their teaching, all their signs and wonders—nothing of all that is any concern of mine.

For me the sign is the eternal unrest in my soul. Of course I ought to have let him lean his head against my house. But to me he was no god, but just a criminal—one of the many who dragged themselves by with their cross, with whom no one would have anything to do. Compassion? Love of mankind? Maybe. But I'm not a loving man, and have never pretended to be. I'm an ordinary person, quite ordinary, like most others. When it happened I was a happy man, carefree and heartless as is natural when one has nothing in particular on one's mind. Wicked perhaps, but not more so than others. Of his doctrine of love I know little—only enough to be sure that it's not for me. And besides, is he himself really so loving? To those who love him he gives peace, they say, and he takes them up with him into his heaven; but they say, too, that he hurls those who don't believe in him into hell. If this is true, then he seems to be exactly like ourselves, just as good and just as bad. Those we love we too treat well, and we wish the rest all the evil there is. If we had the power that he has, we too, perhaps, would hurl them to damnation for all eternity, though we can't be sure. Only the malignity of a god, perhaps, could be great enough for that.

I've come upon these people here and there about the world, but I've never come to know them well. I never get really close to anyone, for they withdraw from me—they're timid, aware, no doubt, of something odd about me, something queer, something that frightens them. I expect it's my eyes that frighten them. I've noticed that people look away if their eyes meet mine. They daren't look into them—into these dried-up wells, these depths with nothing in them. Who is not frightened by such things? It's only natural that they should be.

As she was.

As she . . . By now she will have found men with young eyes, I used to think to myself on my solitary wanderings. And my heart would shrivel and I would hold my hand over my eyes as if to hide them, though there was no one there to see, no one from whom to hide them.

And why should she not? It must be so. When I had young eyes she loved me. Did she?

Thus I thought to myself. But once, far away in a foreign land, I met a man from the city of my birth, who told me that my wife had died in her mother's house—little and wizened and no longer beautiful—and that long before then my son had died of the plague.

So they were gone, the two who had laughed together.

How long ago is that? I cannot tell, for time does not exist for me. Why should it? But it feels a very long time ago.

Yes, they will all die. One generation after another, with their afflictions and crimes and all the things with which they afflict and torment one another. But I shall never die. So long as these creatures exist—evil, most often—I too shall exist, evil myself; their destiny is mine. And that is why I ask about it—why I want to look into it, into the future, although I dread it. Tear down the veil and let me see, however terrible it may be!

He was silent.

Darkness had fallen long before, and from the one to whom he had spoken no answer came. He sat as if alone.

"I have seen god, as you have," *he added after a* time. "I have met him, and the meeting has filled my soul with horror."

The old woman was quite hidden from him in the darkness. But he heard her say in a low, almost tone-less voice: "There is no joy in seeing God."

And she rose, drawing her garment about her as if she were cold. It had indeed grown chilly since sunset and a light shiver ran through him too. When she invited him to go in he followed her, crouching through the low, doorless opening. He had never been in so small a human dwelling before. He could not stand upright and from where he was he could touch every wall; the wall that was the mountain side was dripping with moisture.

She lit the fire, taking fuel from a pile of brushwood and tree roots on the earth floor. The hearth was simply a stone set in this floor, and the smoke escaped through a hole in the slate roof against the mountain wall.

When the fire blazed up he looked about him in that curious room, and to his surprise he saw that they were not alone. Away in a dim corner a gray-haired man was squatting—a man or a child, he could not be sure which; he could not determine, and the uncertainty gave him a sense of something inexplicable, almost frightening; he could not think why this should be, but so it was. The face was like a child's, with a smile which in the half-dark seemed enigmatic —enigmatic perhaps, simply because he could see no reason for it. It was neither a good nor a wicked smile, it appeared altogether detached in its changelessness —perhaps that was what made it seem mysterious— although the eyes in that grizzled, forward-poking head followed their every move. He thought it very strange. For a moment a blurred memory crossed his mind—of what? A memory stirred by this smile? No, he could not capture it, he could not pin it down.

But this gray-headed child crouching in the half-dark with his changeless smile had a singular and frightening effect. He could not take his eyes off it. What sort of a being was it, what sort of secret, in this house which seemed hardly like a human dwelling at all?

"That is my son," said the old woman. "You can speak quite freely before him; he understands nothing."

But the stranger could not bring himself to speak, or to ask about what was now occupying his thoughts —about the son who was to sit there in his corner listening to their conversation without understanding any of it, and smiling that smile . . .

It was the old woman who broke the silence at last, saying, "That was a strange god you met. Was he crucified?"

"Yes."

"Curious. If he was god's son. Why was it?"

"I don't know—I can't make out either what good it was supposed to do. But I've heard it said that it was because he had to suffer. That his father wanted him to suffer. But that's sheer madness; I can't explain it, either to you or to myself."

"A cruel god."

"Yes, indeed. But it's just hearsay. To let a man suffer! What good can that do!"

"I think I recognize that god," she murmured to

herself. And after a while she continued a little hesitantly, "And she who bore god this son—do you know anything of her?"

"No, I never heard anything about her. She was just an ordinary woman, I should think."

"Yes, I imagine so. So you know nothing about her?"

"No. All I heard them say was that by having this child she became god's mother—as of course she would. No, I know nothing about her; why do you ask?"

"I was just wondering what she was like and what sort of life she led. How god treated her while he loved her, and afterwards when perhaps he loved her no more. Whether she was a happy woman, I mean, and whether bearing god's son gave her joy. Or whether he let her be crucified too."

"No, no, of course he didn't! Of course not. And anyhow she was a woman."

"Yes, of course."

She sat silent for a time. Then she asked, "This son—you said he was a god of love?"

"Yes, you could call him that. He preached the love of mankind—all people were to love one another. That's what he meant, I think, if I've rightly understood it."

"What a strange teaching . . . He must be an extraordinary god."

"That may well be."

"I've never heard tell of such a god. Yet I've heard about so many that I thought I knew them all. How happy she must have been . . . It's a pity you don't know anything about her—the one who was allowed to bring him into the world—who was chosen for it."

"I wish he'd never been born. Then I might have lived my life happily, as I did before I met him."

"Aye, aye. It's dangerous to meet a god, as we all know. But why didn't you let him lean his head against your house? Why did you deny him that? Such lovelessness must have been a great crime against him."

"Lovelessness! I am as I am, and I've never pretended to be anything different. I'm like everybody else, and what's wrong with that? And do you think god himself is so full of love? Do you really think so? Has he shown himself so to you? Then why did he curse you . . ."

The old woman made a sharp movement and he broke off. She raked the fire with a half-charred branch and sent the sparks flying upward.

After a while he went on, "You committed a crime against god, and were cursed by him as I was. Why was that? Was he in the right? Is he always right? Are we never in the right against him?"

He looked at her furrowed old face, hoping that she would open her own surely tormented soul to him and let him see into her destiny, which he believed would help him to understand his own. But she just sat looking into the flames, and he knew nothing of what stirred in her.

"That blind beggar down there told me about it, but not so that one could understand what really happened to you.

"How was it that you became priestess of the oracle?" he went on after a pause, hoping that she would at least tell him this.

"My parents were devout people," she replied at last. "That was no doubt the reason. And then we were very poor."

"Poor? Surely you couldn't be made priestess for that?"

"Ah yes, I could. But there's no joy in remembering such things."

"Was it here in Delphi?"

"No, we lived some way down the valley. We were peasants."

"Oh."

"You could see the place from here if it was daytime; it's no further than that. And although my eyes aren't what they were I can make out the gable end, and the old olive tree beside it. But who lives there now I don't know."

"Have you no kinsfolk left?"

"Kinsfolk? I should hardly think so. But how can I know? Kinsfolk? No, those I speak of have been dead a long, long time. . . ."

"You haven't spoken of any."

"No—no, I haven't; that's true . . ."

"But you were thinking of some, perhaps?"

"Yes, I was thinking of my parents, of my mother and father. But how long ago it is—to think that one can remember things that were so long ago . . ."

My father was a good husbandman, but the fields were small and meager; they yielded little, toil as he might—and everything had to be done by hand; he had no draft animals. And of course the fields weren't his own; he had to give most of the crop to the temple, which owned all the land there. It was the god who owned it, one might say; we belonged entirely to the temple and to him. There was little over when all dues had been rendered. But we were content with little, and had never known anything but poverty. Yes, and now after all I've had to undergo I don't think of it as poverty. I remember the fine big olives we used to get, especially from the old tree at the end of the house—for it was old even then; but it's often the old ones that bear the best. I've never tasted anything like them since. Not olives. That too is long ago.

"And was it there you grew up?"

Yes. Two of their children died and I was the only one left. So I had much love during my childhood and youth. All the same, I was alone—that's strange, isn't it? Children can be alone without anyone knowing it, even when they're surrounded by love. Yes, I must have been an odd child, though it didn't show so much at first. I went about on my own, and was hardly ever with others of my age. We lived a little apart, too, though there were other houses not far off. The person I was with most often was my mother. No doubt we were much alike—both serious. We walked and talked with each other as if we were the same age and had the same experience of life. In fact, neither of us knew much about it. She was quite untouched by what is usually called by that name—by all the meanness, malice and confusion which men call life and which they pride themselves on knowing so well. She knew only the simple things: what it was like to bear children and then lose them, what it was like to love a man who had been young and strong and who was growing toil-worn like herself. Such things she knew, and it may be called enough. Her soul was as pure and simple as a tree. She was a tall woman and indeed she resembled a tree, for there was something restful and peaceful about her. We had a tree like that among the fields a little way down the valley—a big, solitary tree which was sacred. Father worshipped it. He went down to it every morning before beginning the day's work. But Mother and I went a little further down the valley and prayed to a spring which always had fresh verdure around its clear waters. It was very holy. If one stood and looked down into it one saw at once that it was divine. One could see every grain of sand at the bottom, and a place where they whirled gently around, moved by an invisible finger of god.

Yes, my parents were very god-fearing; but for them god was springs and trees and sacred groves, not the one up in the temple, who was too great and faraway for them, and to whom they paid their crushing rent. If they ever went up to Delphi—and it happened very seldom—they preferred to visit the modest temple of Gaia, the earth-goddess; it was just a little wooden cabin and reminded them of their own simple way of living. Of god's might and depth and dreadful power over the human soul they had no idea—nor of all the shamelessness surrounding him and his temple.

They ordered their own relationship with god, and in a grove not far from the house we had our own little turf altar which Father had built, and at which he made sacrifice at the great annual festivals for tillers of the soil. But on ordinary days, too, he liked to lay some little gift there when he came back in the evening after his day's work: a few ears of corn from the fields, or fruit and berries of some kind according to the season. And, of course, before and after each meal he made offerings at the hearth, like everyone else; but I can still remember with what reverence he did it, whereas so many others do it thoughtlessly, with no sense of its content or meaning. He was a heavy, taciturn man, and I remember his gentle but always rather sorrowful look and his big, coarse hands, which on the inside were like the bark of an old stone pine. They made me feel so safe when he held me. It was safe and sweet, too, when we went walking together, and my little hand quite disappeared in his. But he seldom said anything. In his later years he grew more and more melancholy, especially after Mother's death. And certainly, too, because of his sorrow at what happened to me. He lived so long that he had to witness it all. I've often wondered whether he, too, cursed me.

He died quite alone. They found him under the tree I spoke of, the one that was sacred; but those who found him didn't know that it was sacred, and therefore couldn't understand why he had lain down under it to die. No funerary sacrifices are offered at his grave, but I hope he is not angry with me on that account and that his soul is nevertheless at peace.

As I grew up it began to be noticed that I was not quite like other girls of my age. I saw visions and heard voices; this was when the signs of womanhood first appeared. Later it passed. Yet I was still abstracted and alien to reality in some way; I began to keep even more to myself than before, and ceased to confide in Mother. I felt my loneliness and my difference from other people more keenly. I could not explain it, but it caused me suffering. And I grew very restless; I felt unsafe, though I was in the midst of safety. That very security began to disturb and oppress me. It was queer: I liked to feel it all about me—indeed I could not do without it—yet it gave me great distress. Unknown to the others I became a stranger to their world, though I lived in it and could have lived nowhere else. What other world had I? None. My parents were the only people who existed for me and I loved them infinitely. Yet I went about my home like a stranger, filled with an unease of which they had no inkling and which, if they had, they would not have understood. They lived on, firm in their simple faith in all about them and in a god who existed in everything that surrounded them.

God? Had I a god any longer? Yes, surely—but where was he? He was so far away, he must have forsaken me. Or had I forsaken him? Had I? Was that it? Why else was I so restless, so bereft of safety? Was not god that very safety—peace and safety? Was he not all the things I no longer possessed?

I had long spells of utter indifference. And yet I burned with a vague longing for I knew not what. And suddenly, without warning and for no reason at all, I would be filled with a glowing wave—a wave of happiness and excitement which at first was glorious but afterwards became so violent and hot that it filled me with anguish and terror, so that I had to press my hand hard against my eyes for a while until the wave subsided and I became myself again. Myself? But who was that?

Who was I?

All this time I was physically sound and healthy, strong and powerfully built like my parents. That was the curious thing. I was a blend of disease and perfect health, of an overstrung creature and an ordinary peasant girl. For this reason my true state was not as noticeable as one might have expected.

In time, of course, it became known that I was a little odd, as indeed all our family were reputed to be. This must have been what made the temple people think of me when they needed a new pythia. I don't remember clearly, but I believe I was about twenty when this happened. Those who ruled and ordained made up their minds that this poor, odd peasant girl who was thought to be rather simple, and whose parents were dependent on the temple and on god, would do very well. Also she came of a pious and very god-fearing home, they had heard, and this was a good thing.

Father and Mother were quite bewildered when the proposal was made to them. They had never imagined such a thing. They realized that it was a great honor—for it was, of course; it was certainly that. And they knew that the god was a great and mighty god who had an incomparable dwelling place: a temple which they must say was very fine and splendid, though they had only been inside it a few times and had felt quite lost there among all the precious things and strange people. Nor could one well refuse the mighty ones up there, the most powerful in all

Delphi. Whatever such men proposed must be right. Though one didn't understand enough about it to know how to answer. They supposed they would have to say yes—to trust in god and hope that it was he who wished it, anxious though it made them to hand me over to something they knew nothing whatever about.

And I? I myself?

I was strangely troubled when I heard of it. Chosen? Was I chosen? Summoned to the temple? To god?

Chosen to be his instrument, to speak his words—words inspired by him—I to be filled with his spirit, seized by holy rapture?

I? I chosen for this?

It aroused a tumult in me; it frightened me, annihilated me—and filled me with boundless happiness.

Was it possible? Could *I* be wanted by god? But they said so, they believed so. By god, who had forsaken me. Whom I had forsaken. Could such a thing come about? Was I chosen by him to be his handmaid, his prophetess, would he speak through my mouth? It was inconceivable—a miracle. Was it the miracle I had been awaiting?

No, god had not forgotten me, not forsaken me; nor I him—no, that never. He called me and I came; I came with my whole heart already filled with him.

God was calling me!

When the first feverish excitement had passed I

went about in quiet joy, thinking only of the wonder that awaited me. Now I should know peace and security again, with him.

Mother and I were to go up to the temple together. We went one morning, and when we had made known our errand we were shown into a house by the temple court, and taken before the man who at that time held the highest priestly office. This was an elderly man, a member of one of the foremost families in Delphi, and we had never met such a person before. He was kind, and it was really not at all difficult. He asked a few questions about our way of life and then talked to me for a time, asking me about my childhood and other things which I couldn't think why he should want to know about; and he seemed satisfied with my presumably artless replies. At last he told me that the god dwelling in this temple was the god of light, that he was the greatest of all gods and his oracle the most eminent of any in the world. To be its priestess, called and initiated by the god himself, was a signal grace and a great responsibility. I stared down at the floor with my mind in a turmoil and full of happiness.

Then he summoned a servant, who led us across the open court into the temple, and handed us over to a priest who was now to take charge of us.

I had never been in the temple before. And while Mother stood there, simple and foreign to it all like any countrywoman, without looking about her very much, I gazed around enraptured, overwhelmed by the wealth and magnificence of this holy room. I had never seen anything like it before and could never even have imagined its existence. I was seized with reverence and joy to be standing here in the presence of the divine. Yes, this was indeed the temple of the god of light, the god's own abode, the house in which he dwelt.

The priest seemed pleased with my delight and also, it seemed, to know that strangely enough I had never been in there before. He let me stand undisturbed in my adoration. Then he led us further into the sanctuary, to its very heart. A narrow door led into another room, and here he told Mother to stay outside and wait for us. We entered the room, which was not very large, and he told me that this was where the pilgrims assembled—those who came to consult the oracle. Then we went down a narrow stairway into an almost completely dark room, lit only by two feeble oil lamps. The air here was oppressive and musty, almost suffocating, and I felt I could hardly breathe. The floor was uneven and slimy and I realized that it was the wet, living rock itself. In it there was a crevice, over which stood a tall tripod flanked by two high bowls; or so I thought, but I couldn't discern anything clearly. And I saw no walls; the place was just a sort of pit in the ground, full of queer smells—a sickly blend of fragrance and stifling fumes that seemed to be rising from the rift in the rock and, much to my surprise, a faint, sour smell of goat. I was shaken; I breathed shallowly, panting, and once I almost thought I was going to faint.

The priest who, despite the darkness, seemed to be observing me closely, explained that this was the holy of holies where god spoke, where he inspired the pythia with what she should utter in her delirium; it was here that he would fill me with his spirit. I panted and could not answer. He seemed satisfied with me and with the impression the holy room had made upon my sensitive mind. And when he had forbidden me ever to hint at anything I had seen or might see, we turned back again. With my hand pressed hard against my eyes, as my way was when disturbed, I followed him up the narrow stairs.

Mother seemed to have been waiting for us with some uneasiness, and she looked at me searchingly when I rejoined her. I was still breathing heavily, but hoped she wouldn't notice it. I looked about me with empty eyes in that great bright temple where the sunshine was pouring in exactly as before. But I felt no gladness now. And for a time, as if too full of something else, I closed my eyes against the light. It was as if for the first time I had sensed something of god.

We parted from the priest in the entrance hall. He told me when to come again, and Mother and I went home in silence, side by side. She asked what he had shown me, but I answered evasively, and we went the whole way home without another word.

I had to be alone with this as with everything else; with the knowledge that god was incomprehensible, inconceivable—that he dwelt in a hole in the ground —that he frightened me! And yet that I longed for him. For I did, I did in spite of everything, and although he was not at all as I had expected, and would hardly help me as I had thought he would. Though he was only calling me.

Why me? Why should I of all people be the chosen one?

He had a temple up in the daylight, too, it was true. A beautiful, glorious temple. But from what they told me it was not the holiest place, and it was not there that I was to serve him. It was not there that he was waiting to fill me with his spirit. There he was another being and had no use for me. For it was not with his light that he meant to fill my soul. Down in a hole beneath the sanctuary he would reveal himself to me, and I would be possessed by god.

And yet—I longed to be there! Despite my fears, my terror of what awaited me, I longed only to be there! I thought of nothing else, never of anything but of being shut into that musty, stifling, suffocating hole, to prophesy with wide-open mouth, to shriek out wild, incomprehensible words through frothing lips, filled with his spirit; to be used, made use of by my god!

In this excitement I waited for what was to come. But in time the excitement subsided and was followed by a kind of lethargy in which I lived and moved; inwardly I was seething still, though the tumult never broke out. I don't know if those who now took charge of me noticed this—noticed my condition. I was often up there, for the feast day upon which I was to become pythia was approaching and they wanted to prepare me for my task and keep me under their influence, away from my parents. I grasped little of these preparations, and in some I could see no purpose at all; some years had passed, I remember, before I understood that some nasty thing they did to me was to find out whether I was a virgin. I lived in another world than theirs; perhaps god had plunged me into this lethargy to protect me, to keep me living in his world and not in theirs. It is possible, though I know nothing about it.

The seventh day of the spring month, which is god's day, was drawing near, and it was then that I was to be pythia for the first time. I was the only one they could turn to, for the woman who had been pythia before me had died quite suddenly sometime earlier, in circumstances which they did not want known. They were expecting many pilgrims to come for the festival, which lasted several days, and they were uneasy about my performance, since I had never done it before—about whether god would speak through me and whether I could endure the intense strain for so many days on end. They were full of consideration and care. But not on my account; I realized that even then, though I was like a child and had

hardly ever been out among people before and knew
almost nothing about them. I understood, too, that
they lived not for god but for his temple—that it was
the temple they loved and not him—and for its prestige and renown in the world. Great flocks of pilgrims
would certainly be coming to this god's most solemn
festival as usual, bringing the temple many gifts
which would still further increase its wealth and
power. All the inns were expected to be full and
everyone in the city would profit in one way or another by what was to take place. These feasts which
brought visitors from all over the world meant much
to the people here; indeed, it was by them they lived.
The whole city was preparing to receive the guests.

I didn't understand this then; I knew nothing
about it, but later I was to know it all too well. I was
to learn what manner of thing surrounded god and
his holy place and what his fame meant to the people
in all these houses that clung to the mountain round
about the temple like a swarming ant hill. Because of
their association with god and because they did no
mundane work, they considered themselves to be in
a privileged position, and, in fact, looked down upon
the strangers who made their way to this remarkable
community in the mountains. They were very proud
of their city and regarded it as holy, because everyone
in it lived on god.

But all this was still hidden from me; I noticed a
great commotion but gave it no thought, and in a way

did not see it. I went about in my daze, into which god himself had perhaps plunged me, seemingly untouched by anything outside.

The day came, god's day, with which his festival opened, and I remember that morning very well. Never was there such a sunrise over these mountains— never, at least, that I have seen. I had fasted for three days and was light, weightless as a bird. I bathed in Castalia's spring; the water was fresh and I felt pure— freed from all that did not belong to god's morning. They dressed me as a bride—his bride—and I walked slowly along the sacred way to the temple. People must have been massed all along the wayside and in the open court itself, but I never noticed them or knew that they were there. I existed only for god. And I walked up the steps of the temple where one of his servants sprinkled me with holy water, and stepped into his radiant sanctuary, into all the brightness where he was not waiting for me, where I might not serve him. I walked through it with the tears burning under my closed eyelids—for I shut my eyes not to see his glory and perhaps fail him—fail in the task which he had given me to do and for which he had chosen me. Led between two priests I passed the altar where his eternal fire was burning, entered the pilgrims' hall and went down the narrow, dim stairway into the holy of holies.

There was as little light there as before and it was some time before I could make out anything. But I noticed the stifling fumes from the cleft at once, and they seemed even more stifling and swooning than before. I smelt the stench of goat, too, but this time it was much stronger and more pungent. I could not explain it. There must have been something burning there, for I could smell that as well. And then after a while I saw a glow in a bowl in the darkness, and a little man was crouching over it, fanning life into the embers with a bird's wing that looked like a kite's. A yellow-gray snake writhed past his foot and vanished swiftly in the darkness. This filled me with terror, for I had heard it whispered that the former pythia died from the bite of such a snake, but I had not believed it, and I had seen no snakes when I was there before. Later I learned that it was true; that they were always there and were much venerated, because they were oracle beasts and had divine understanding. I also learned that the embers glowing in the bowl were pieces of laurel: the god's sacred tree, whose smoke the priestess must inhale to be filled with his spirit.

Now the little man rose up from his bowl and his bird's wing and looked at me so kindly that my terrors were a little allayed. His dry, wizened face was good-natured and he even smiled at me a little. I didn't know then that he was to be my only friend in the sanctuary, my help and consolation through the years, and especially when fate swooped down upon me like an eagle from its cleft. In my present drowsy state I took little note of him, but I felt that he was not like the others and that he meant me nothing but good, although he had to attend to his work here. It was he who now handed me a bowl of fresh laurel leaves, recently plucked in the god's sacred grove; these I must chew, together with ashes, for this too would fill me with his spirit. And it was then that the little servant of the oracle smiled at me, as if to calm my fears, and among all these frightening things his smile was kind and reassuring. But of course he said nothing to me, for here in the holiest place no one might speak.

What he gave me tasted horrible; and whether because of its effect on me or because of my exhaustion after fasting, I felt ill, and reeled a little. The two priests of the oracle who were watching me the whole time helped me up onto the tripod, which was too high for me to mount unaided; then they set the dish of embers on a high stand, bringing it to a level with my head, and with every breath I had to inhale the drugging smoke. It was acrid and produced a peculiar giddiness. But it was the fumes rising from the cleft in the rock which affected me most, for I was far more aware of them now that I was sitting directly over them: they were poisonous and nauseous. It was horrible, and the thought flashed through my mind that the cleft was believed by some to run right down into the realms of death, from which the oracle really drew its power; for death knows all things. I was seized with horror at having this beneath me, horror of losing consciousness and perhaps sinking and being engulfed in it—horror of the realms of death—the realms of death . . . I felt myself sinking, sinking . . . But where was god, where was god! He was not there, he was not coming to me. He was not filling me with his spirit as he had promised. I was only sinking, sinking . . .

With my senses quite clouded, half conscious, I dimly saw one of the priests of the oracle leading forward from the obscurity a he-goat with unusually large horns; it seemed to me that he poured water over its head. Then I knew no more.

But all at once everything changed. I felt relief, release; a feeling not of death but of life, life—an indescribable feeling of delight, but so violent, so unprecedented . . . It was he! He! It was he who filled me, I felt it, I knew it! He was filling me, he was annihilating me and filling me utterly with himself, with his happiness, his joy, his rapture. Ah, it was wonderful to feel his spirit, his inspiration coming upon me—to be his, his alone, to be possessed by god. By his ecstasy, his happiness, by the wild joy that was in god. Is there anything more wonderful than sharing god's delight in being alive.

But the feeling mounted and mounted; it was still full of delight and joy but it was too violent, too overpowering, it broke all bounds—it broke me, hurt me, it was immeasurable, demented—and I felt my body beginning to writhe, to writhe in agony and torment; being tossed to and fro and strangled, as if I were to be suffocated. But I was not suffocated, and instead I began to hiss forth dreadful, anguished sounds, utterly strange to me, and my lips moved without my will; it was not I who was doing this. And I heard shrieks, loud shrieks; I didn't understand them, they were quite unintelligible, yet it was I who uttered them. They issued from my gaping mouth, though they were not mine. . . . It was not myself at all, I was no longer I, I was his, his alone; it was terrible, terrible and nothing else!

How long it went on I don't know. I had no sense of time while it was happening. Nor do I know how I afterwards got out of the holy of holies or what happened next; who helped me and took care of me. I awoke in the house next to the temple where I lived during this time, and they said I had lain in a deep sleep of utter exhaustion. And they told me that the priests were much pleased with me and that I had exceeded all their hopes as priestess of the oracle. The old woman with whom I lived told me this, and then she left me to have a thorough rest.

I lay there in my bridal gown, as god's bride. It was the only bridal gown I would ever wear. And I remember feeling the fine, strange fabric, and being very lonely.

God? Who was god? And where was he now? Why

was he not here? No longer with me? Where was he, my bridegroom? Why had he forsaken me?

I didn't understand him. But I longed for him. No, I didn't understand him at all, I didn't know at all who he was—less than ever since I had been his, since he had filled me with his spirit, with his bliss, his rapture, until I screamed with pain. Yes, he had filled me with agony. Nevertheless I longed for him, and him only. For without him all was nothingness and void.

Suppose he were to come here to me from his temple, where no doubt he was now being worshipped by his people, by all those who adored him there for his glory's sake! If he were to come and take me in his arms, as lovers surely do, afterwards. Not let me lie here quite alone in my bridal gown, as if forsaken by him, by my beloved, now that he had no further use for me—now that I had fulfilled my task, and to his satisfaction. Now that the fever, the delirium, the possession was over. Why did he love me only then! Why was he with me only then!

How gladly I would have rested quite still in his embrace, without raving or any excitement. Just rested safely and happily in his arms.

Or did I not want this? Was this not what I longed for?

It was, it was. But should I ever experience it? Was I meant for that—was it for that he wanted to use me?

Security. Peace. How could I desire such things? How could I believe I could find such things in his embrace? How could I ask security of god?

God could not be as I wished him to be, as I so much wanted him to be. He could not. God was not security and repose and rest. He was unrest, conflict and uncertainty. Those things were god.

I lay and watched dusk darkening in the room. He had plunged me into so deep a sleep that it was now evening—the day was over.

In the morning, early in the morning, as soon as the sun rose above the mountains my bridegroom would come to me, he would fill me again with his spirit, his hot breath, his bliss, and I should be his once more!

So began my life as his priestess—my long service with him.

I lived sometimes at home, sometimes in the house by the temple, with the old woman who had charge of me. She had always tended the pythia during the great festivals. For the festivals were many and long, and the service of the oracle was so exhausting that the prophetess had to be cared for by someone; she had to rest thoroughly afterwards and at night have a quiet and strengthening sleep. A great part of the old woman's life had been spent in this work, under the direction of the priests. She knew all about the pythias from a long time back, and liked to talk of them. She always wanted to talk. She knew all about the

priests, too—what they were like, which of them
really believed and which only pretended. I learned
at once that the one who first led me into the holy of
holies only pretended; yet he was greatly respected,
for as treasurer he had done much for the temple.
His period of office was now nearly at an end; appointments were held for a fixed number of years.
All came of good families in Delphi. Those in the
highest positions were drawn from the most eminent
families; and of these she talked often and in great
detail. In her eyes it seemed to be this fact which
gave the temple its real prestige. The sanctuary and
all concerning it lay very close to her heart and she
was evidently extremely proud of her position there.
Of god I never heard her speak.

Despite her respect for the men in high places and
their birth, she never spoke well of them—no, not
even of them. She never spoke a really good word for
anyone, but she had a keen eye for human failings.
The image of the world that I, so young and inex-
perienced, gained through her was warped and dis-
torted; I felt this, yet I could see that much of it was
true and it puzzled and bewildered me. I have often
thought that this woman, whom I came to loathe
and despise so heartily, did more to form my views
of mankind than anyone else, and made them bitter
and unjust. Despite my loathing of her and my con-
viction that she was wrong, she did influence me. And
at last, by revealing herself to me in all her vileness,

she confirmed me in my belief that her false idea of human beings was the right one. Thus we gather knowledge which we call truth from those in whom we least believe, and unconsciously let ourselves be led by what we most heartily detest.

Later I myself experienced much human malignity, and added it to what I had absorbed from her. But now, after sitting up here in my solitude for so long, thinking of all I went through, I've often asked myself, in spite of what was done to me: Are men really so wicked? Has not my own bitter destiny led me astray in my judgment of them? I don't know, for I never meet anyone now. But in my loneliness I have thought so.

She influenced me because so much of what she said was true. She was speaking the truth when she told me of the baseness of the holy city and the licentiousness attending the great festivals. All these men from every corner of the world had to have light women, and all the poor girls in the place—and not only the poor ones, either—were procured for them by the agency of the inns. There were few virgins in Delphi, she declared—and that must have been why I had been chosen as pythia, she blurted out suddenly, making me quite red and confused; and then she said no more of that. And there were the rogues and cheats who were attracted by the fairground life of the great festivals, and all the shady and dishonest dealing that went on under the very wing of the temple. There were scoundrels even among the priests, who took bribes for giving the desired answers from the oracle and for giving the pythia's utterances the desired interpretation—though she had to admit that this was rare—or who kept the money paid over at the sacrifices, or made profits for themselves by selling the skins of sacrificial animals, and so on; all kinds of ways of cheating the temple were open to those who held the right appointments in it and, so far as she knew, many—even perhaps most—people took advantage of such opportunities.

I must say that her nasty talk and the falsehood and meanness of what she told me, and what I unhappily had many chances of observing for myself, all around me, gave me a very lofty idea of god, and love for him. If he was surrounded by such corruption—if he arose from such a morass as this—he was the more extraordinary, the more worthy to be loved. And it was necessary to love him. For what else was there in this dirty world to love but him? And what desolation it was to be tossed out into it as I had been, tossed out into this detestable world of men.

I longed to leave her evil prattling and everything else behind me and return to him—to him whom she never mentioned; I was thankful that she did not. I longed for his embrace, for the dark hole in the ground where he would enfold me in his arms and fill me with his heavenly ecstasy, his wild bliss, his spirit.

His spirit? And what was his spirit? Was it simply sublimity and greatness? Exaltation? Only that?

If so, if it were as simple as that, why was it such anguish to be his? Why need I suffer agony and shriek with pain? Why was his love not gentleness and peace as I so longed for it to be? Why did it bring me no safety, never the safety for which I prayed continually, from my innermost heart? He was wonder, release—why must he be also terrible and frightening and cruel and immense—why so many things at once—why did he strangle me at the moment of bliss, and leave me forsaken when he seemed nearest and I most needed him?

Who was he? Who?

I threw myself into his arms, wild and fevered like himself, and before he stunned me and annihilated me with his immensity I cried: God, who are you, who are you? But he never answered.

He filled me with himself, erased me with himself, but who he was he did not reveal.

He never did. To this day I sit here in my loneliness and think about him, wondering who he is. I ask still, but he does not answer.

Yes, I loved him. I loved him with all my heart. But my love did not make me happy. It was not that kind of love.

But I was going to talk about the old woman. To me she was always good and kind, and she praised me in exaggerated terms. The priests had told her

that I was the best pythia they had had for a very long
time, she said, and among all those whom she had
had living with her not one could be compared with
me. She spoke very contemptuously of these prede-
cessors of mine; it was painful to hear her talk so of
these women, whom I could not think of without
sympathy and a sense of fellowship. I had seen one
or two of them in the streets of Delphi; especially
one thin, queer woman who slunk along the rows of
houses mumbling to herself incessantly. The old
woman laughed heartily at this one, making fun of
the fact that she had lost what little wits she ever had,
but I listened with a shudder, reflecting that I too
might come to the same end.

It was a long time before I realized that it was as
priestesses that she despised them. For other reasons,
too, certainly, but above all because they had been
pythias, for this she thought contemptible in itself.

I was astounded. Could she be serious? Yes, there
was no doubt about it. She did not say so directly, to
be sure, but for all that it was plain enough. I cannot
say how amazed I was to discover this.

And now that my eyes were opened at last I found
that she was not alone in her opinion. I began no-
ticing those about me—their treatment of me, their
behavior to me—and I understood ever more clearly
that it was as she had hinted and that I held a despised
position among mankind. People avoided me. Yes, I
had noticed that long before, and realized that it

arose from timidity, a dread of someone who had been in such close touch with the divine, which as everyone knows is a dangerous matter—of one who was sometimes possessed by god and whose shrieks in the secret pit below the ground could at times be heard up in the temple. People hung back from me, and I didn't wonder at it—but now I saw that they also looked down on me: they regarded me as a sort of outcast and preferred to ignore me. I kept myself to myself always, and liked best to be alone as had been my way from a child; but now it dawned on me that in fact no one wanted to be with me or have anything to do with me—that my solitude was enforced and real.

It is strange how depressed and sad this made me. Although I cared nothing for company and wanted none, although I seemed born to loneliness, nevertheless it saddened me. And when young people in the street nudged one another and whispered as I passed, it cut me to the quick, though I didn't really understand why it should.

Did they despise me too? They probably never thought about it, but they must have felt that I was different.

Yes, and I was. I was not like them. Not young, as they were.

Young? I wasn't really much older than they. But young? Young?

They never spoke to me. No one did, unless it was really necessary.

Even the priests who praised me so—for they did praise me, both to my face and to others—and valued me for the sake of the oracle, never said anything to me beyond what was needful for my service, and for my tasks in connection with it. They were interested in me only as a pythia, as one employed in the sanctuary; I had no other existence for them. And without ever saying a harsh word—rather, indeed, by a constant condescending kindness—they showed that there was a gulf fixed between them and this poor ignorant girl from a poor family somewhere down the valley. They appreciated me and prized me as a good pythia—one through whom god clearly liked to speak and whom he filled at once with his mighty spirit—but although this meant that I was of great service to them and although I was chosen by god, they looked upon me as they always looked upon those so employed. They felt nothing but a sort of pitying contempt for this poor, raving, half-conscious woman whom they set upon the tripod in the god's stifling pit. Her inspiration was divine, no doubt, but it was they who interpreted it and knew how to extract a meaning from confused utterance which was unintelligible to everyone else. The great thoughts, the lofty wisdom which they put into the oracle's answers—those famous answers which conferred world-wide power and prestige upon the oracle—had nothing to do with the wild shrieks of this ignorant woman; or very little. She was possessed by god, certainly: god spoke through her. But it was they who knew what god really meant and wanted to say—they who knew how to penetrate the core of him and reveal it.

And it was true. I had no share in this, in their wise interpretations of his message; I was altogether shut out. I didn't know what I said, what I screamed in my delirium, my possession; their manner of interpretation and exploitation had nothing to do with me. I was simply filled with god.

I didn't know what he put into me, I knew nothing of his wisdom, I really knew nothing at all about him, nor guessed who he might be. I was simply filled with him. I only felt him in me. I was his. No more.

But was this so contemptible? I could not see it. To be filled with god—how could they feel such profound contempt for this? I did not understand.

What I had taken to be a divine grace, an election, a call from him to be his chosen one, his priestess, the one through whose mouth he spoke, they regarded as somehow degrading. Degrading to be the elect of god!

The oracle was said to command veneration throughout the world; yet the one into whom god injected his spirit, in whom he took up his abode, was an outcast with whom no one would come in contact or even speak.

I was baffled.

The woman with whom I lived, who was honest in her own peculiar way, told me how fortunate it was that they had found me, since it was so difficult to find anyone willing to be pythia. Not even the poorest would be pythia now. And she hinted that no one but my poor, simple-minded parents, who lived all on their own in the valley and were a little queer in the head, could have been persuaded to consent to it.

I was utterly confounded. You can well imagine how it troubled and oppressed me, and how many fearful thoughts it aroused in me.

Chosen? Suppose after all I had not been chosen? Or not by god, only by the priests, who perhaps didn't even believe in him. Suppose what she said was true and they had only taken me from my poor ignorant parents by guile, because they could get no one else? Suppose god had not called me at all, and I was not his elect, his chosen?

I had believed myself to be so, and I had felt myself seized by his spirit, filled with him, I thought. But was it so? Was it quite certainly so? How could I tell! Certainly I had felt myself to be one with him—I had felt myself full of his glory; yet immediately afterwards I was quite forsaken and alone and he was not with me at all. Almost always I was forsaken by him, filled only by a boundless void. I longed for him but he was indifferent; I cried out for him but he made no reply. I asked: Who are you? But he did not tell me. You whom I love above all else! But he gave me no answer. Never any answer.

Until he came to me again, hurled himself upon me again like a storm of savage heat, rapture, bliss. At such times I was happy—happier than all other people in the world—everything was right and perfect—for a little while. Then I was cast down into emptiness again. Into an emptiness which no one else had ever had to feel—not as I felt it—I who had been his, who had shared god's vast joy at being alive.

Thus it was for me. Thus was my love for god—and I did not even know who he was.

It gave me no security, no assurance, no certainty. I could never rest quietly in his embrace. Heat and rapture I felt, but never stillness and serenity. I prayed for it, but he never gave it me.

Can it be so if one is the elect of god?

I kept these thoughts to myself as usual. Whom could I share them with, in whom could I confide? The only one who could have helped me and answered my questions was more remote than ever before; I had never felt so far from him as during this time. I longed to throw myself into his arms—I longed only for that—yet at the same time I dreaded it; for the first time I was full of fear—fear of the day

when once more I should be decked as a bride and led
down into his pit—down into the holy of holies to
meet him.

I had long to wait, for no festival was near. Then an
oracle day was fixed upon between festivals, as was
sometimes done when pilgrims were expected. The
morning came; I bathed in Castalia's spring and was
dressed in my bridal gown. I walked up the sacred
way, passed through the temple and down the dim
stair as usual. All was as usual in the cave, and I
breathed the air greedily: the smoke from the smol-
dering laurel, the acrid goat-stench, the sickening
fumes from the cleft under the tripod—all that could
drug me, excite me, deliver me into his embrace.
Burning with desire for him I sat with eyes closed,
with the taste of the leaves from his sacred tree in
my mouth, waiting to be filled with him again—with
his living spirit, his painful delight and bliss; waiting
for him to erase me and all my longing and my doubt,
and bring all to consummation.

But he did not come. He did not come. I inhaled
the vapors in deep, eager drafts, and felt them working in me—felt that I was near to stifling and swooning. But they had no other effect on me. I was not inspired by god, and I did not feel his presence.

They brought forward the goat, his sacred beast;
they poured water on its head—and it was then, at
that moment, that his spirit was supposed to come
upon me. But the animal simply lowered its head to

the ground with a queer, whining cry, and then dragged itself back to its obscurity. The priest of the oracle gave in, thinking it useless to try any longer.

I sat there with staring eyes, my dry, quivering lips parted for a cry that never came. I was quite empty, with an emptiness and desolation I had never known before, though I had felt something like it often enough. There was emptiness all about me, too, as if there were nothing there; and when I stretched out my hand before me it was as if I stretched it into perfect vacancy and boundless desolation. Only the fumes from the kingdom of death rose up around me, enveloping me in their icy chill.

They had to help me down from the tripod, and when they let go of me I reeled and almost fell. The only one who noticed this was the little servant of the oracle; he hurried up and supported me. I stood leaning against the doorpost until I had mastered the dizziness that had seized me, and seized me in vain.

The priest of the oracle—the one who had first shown me the holy of holies—was much displeased with me, and displeased too because he had to dismiss, with their errand unfulfilled, those who were waiting in the pilgrims' hall. They were only simple country folk, to be sure, who had come to consult the oracle about their everyday cares and worries. Nevertheless he was annoyed on the temple's account that I had failed and been unreceptive to god's inspiration. He used no harsh words, yet his feelings were

plain. He did not believe in god, yet he was angry because I had not been filled with him as usual.

But what was his displeasure compared to my own
despair at what had happened—to the abyss into
which I had been hurled? Now I knew that I had
been forsaken by god, utterly forsaken. Now it was no
longer a matter of uncertainty and unrest, but of certainty. He did not care about me and wanted to have
nothing to do with me. And had he ever cared? Had I
ever been summoned, chosen by him as I had fancied?
And I had believed that he had called for me! Had he
ever wanted me as his instrument, his elect, his priestess?

The priests had wanted me, yes. They had wanted
a poor foolish woman to use in his service. But god
himself had never wanted her. When they forced her
upon him he took her to himself and flung her away
again. He had shown his contempt for the peasant girl,
whom they had brought to him in the belief that he
would accept her and fill her with his holy spirit, love
her as she loved him. Violated and tossed aside . . .
It was for this that I had been chosen.

Called for me? He had never called for me; how
could I have imagined it? It was I who in my loneliness, my abandonment, had called upon him.

In my despair I tortured myself with these bitter,
hopeless thoughts. I believe I should have broken
down altogether had it not been for the little servant
of the oracle. He comforted me and reasoned with

me; he took it more sensibly than I did. Such a thing was bound to happen at times, he said; and he had long experience of the oracle pit. It happened to all pythias, and quite often, and it had to happen to me, too, sooner or later. It didn't mean that god had forsaken his chosen one; certainly not. But at times like these the priest of the oracle was always annoyed, for he was concerned about the reputation of the oracle, as was only natural; and he probably found it vexing that it should occur on the day he was on duty. But god was not angry—not in the least; that was not the reason. No one could really tell what the reason was; no human being could ever know. That was the secret of the oracle pit and it was never revealed.

He himself had had a vague feeling that things were not quite as usual that day—not quite as they should be. Why, he could not say, but he had seen it all so often and could usually feel these things. He had sensed it as soon as he went down into the holy of holies, long before I came. He had scented it, as it were, beforehand. And then the little gray and yellow snakes had not shown themselves—they had not emerged from the secret crevices; and that was a bad sign, a very bad sign. And the goat, the god's sacred beast of which he had charge and which he looked after between oracle days, had behaved queerly that morning when he led it from its stall to the oracle hole; it had bleated and struggled, as if unwilling to go. So what with one thing and another, he had felt that nothing would go right and that there would be no oracle today.

But it was no fault of mine; certainly not. I was in no way to blame. I was a very fine pythia and must surely be much beloved of god. It was clear that he liked to talk through me: he came to me so quickly and I slipped so easily into the proper receptive state. During the ecstasy my face showed that I was filled with him. Anyone who had been there as long as he had could tell that at once.

Thus he talked to me and brought me gradually to a calmer, more reasonable frame of mind. His words, his very nature, and his little face with its kindly wrinkles had a beneficent and calming effect on me. And I should have been even calmer if I had known that at the next festival all would go well once more, and just as usual.

In time I came to realize that it might have been because I had felt anxious, uncertain and doubtful about my meeting with god, and because I had feared it. That must be wrong. One ought not to feel uneasiness, hesitancy or doubt in one's soul, for then one could scarcely be received into his arms.

Yet how could one be without dread, without doubts? How could one approach god without them?

This I did not confide to my friend. I never really confided in him at all. It might sadden him, I thought.

We became very good friends during this time, and remained so as long as I was with the oracle.

We suited one another well, for he, too, was despised. But I believe he never gave that a thought—was never even aware of it—whereas I was troubled by it. Why should I have been? No one had so modest a position in the temple as he, yet it contented him; no one could have been more content than he was. He swept the floor of the temple and the steps outside, he sprinkled water and then with his broom swept out all the dirt that the visitors had brought in. He kept the place clean for god. And he did this most conscientiously; it was always beautifully neat and clean. This was his main task, but he had many others. He tended the laurel trees in the god's sacred grove; he replenished the bowls of holy water at the entrance to the temple; he fed the venomous little oracle snakes with birds' eggs and mice; he carried wood for the eternal fire on god's altar in the sanctuary and made sure that it never went out; for although this was not his responsibility, yet it was he who saw to it. He made sure that all was in order in the holy of holies, and on oracle days he served and helped there as I have described. He was put to every kind of task. He won small thanks. The priests treated him with condescension and often scolded him, except for the senior ones who never addressed him at all. Were one to judge by the treatment he received, one would fancy him almost useless; but in fact he did his work very scrupulously and I'm sure that god was well pleased with him. He more than anyone loved and

venerated the temple; it was the apple of his eye. But
he loved god, too, though not in any ceremonious
manner and not by talking about him very much; he
loved him as he loved his work, his situation, his clean-
ing duties, whose importance he well understood. He
looked after god's house and was ever busy with some
work or other for him. He had a great deal to do with
him, but no problems or troubles ever arose between
them; there was only mutual trust and kindness. No
great distance divided them, and inferior though his
position was he was never anxious or uncertain, but
felt himself to be close to god—a good friend of his.
He associated with him unaffectedly, and all was natural and easy between them.

It was pleasant to see how he lived, to feel the
serenity that surrounded him and in some sort to
share in it. I think he was the happiest person I ever
met. He knew there was purpose in all he did, and he
was good friends with god.

Little wonder, then, if he paid no attention to the
opinions of men or to their treatment of him; and in
any case, as I said, he noticed nothing wrong with it.
He was so ingenuous, so utterly without suspicion and
without perception of human beings as to be quite
touching; at times one could almost have laughed at
him for it. Friendly and smiling he wandered among
them all, including those who never showed him any
kindness in return. He lived for his simple, menial
tasks with a simple, everyday piety of which he him-

self was quite unconscious. He was so devout that he never even knew it.

How well I remember him, long ago though it is. I remember that the soles of his feet were always coal-black, for the sacred place might not be entered save with bare feet, and he was constantly in it, so that the grime became ingrained and never wore off. Whenever he bustled about in there in his eager way, one saw the black soles of his feet.

He is the only one of those down there in the temple whom I remember with gladness; yes, and I find it still does me good to think about him. He must have died long ago.

At the next great festival, as I said, all went well from the first day, largely because he helped me. The evening before he sat with me and talked reassuringly and encouragingly, and then when the time came in the morning and I felt anxious and tense again it was he who made me completely forget it. When he handed me the bowl of leaves to chew he whispered to me softly that the little oracle snakes had come out of their crannies, and he smiled contentedly with all his wrinkles; next he coaxed me into my trance and then into the rapture, the possession which I so longed to feel. Afterwards it was seldom that the ecstasy failed me, but when it did it was always just as terrible as the first time.

They became increasingly pleased with me, and as the years went by it began to be said of me, as the blind beggar told you, that I was the best pythia they had ever had—though that can't be true—and that god would not speak through anyone but me. This was because once when they tried another woman, to ease my burden during the lengthy festivals, she had no success and I had to go on bearing it alone as before.

The regard in which I was held led to my staying on with the oracle as priestess, instead of leaving it after a few years as was usual—usual, because for one thing most of them lacked the strength to continue longer. It was good to have a pythia with such a reputation as mine, and they didn't want to lose me. Nor did I want to leave the temple and its service. The oracle pit and all connected with it held me captive; everything that happened to me there—my transformation into something other than myself, the wildness, the possession, the transcending of all bounds—was something I could no longer be without. I could no longer live without it.

I was also accorded more respect because I had become so well known as a pythia, because everyone knew I was of service to the temple of the oracle and therefore to the town, and because I was considered to be chosen by god in an especial manner. But this very fact made people shyer of me than ever, and indeed I seemed to inspire them with a kind of fear. They avoided me more than before and I was completely shut out from all human society. All knew in what a fearful relationship I stood to god, and how terrible my face was when he filled me with himself. It made me lonelier than any other person in the holy city.

No one saw me as anything but the priestess of the oracle; did I myself? I was one with the oracle and had no life of my own, no existence but in and through it. Yes, I was a pythia only, and no longer a person in the usual meaning of the word.

I now lived almost entirely in Delphi, at the temple's expense, and seldom visited my parents and my home in the valley. I had become quite strange to them and I felt that they were as shy of me as every one else. When I visited them and we started to talk to each other, we seemed not to know what to talk about. Of my life we could say nothing; they didn't understand it and were troubled by hearing of it. And there was so little to be said about their life, we felt; it glided by just as before—just as it had always done —and I knew it inside out. Or did I? Did I know it any longer?

I had become a stranger to their world, and remote from it. Although I could see that it was exactly as it had been before and therefore familiar to me, I was still a stranger there. Nothing is more foreign than the world of one's childhood when one has truly left it.

They were old now, both of them, and they showed it. They moved more slowly and Mother had grown very thin. She looked about her with sunken eyes like an old bird. And she liked to sit and rest in silence. We had so little to say to one another.

I myself was no longer young. How old was I when Mother died? Well up in the thirties, I should think.

A message was sent to the temple to say that she was dying, but they could not give it me at once, for I was just on my way to the holy of holies, and if I had known of it I could not have performed my task and received god's inspiration. I had first to do my duty to the temple and to him. And on that particular day there were exceptionally many pilgrims; it was the last day of the great spring festival and the oracle went on for an unusually long time. The little oracle servant whispered the news to me as soon as I showed signs of coming around, but I was still in my exaltation, my trance, and found it hard at first to grasp what he was saying; it seemed so remote and somehow irrelevant. Gradually I took it in, however, and hurried home in agitation.

I was still dazed when I arrived hot and out of breath at the house, where an infinite stillness reigned. It was always quiet there, but now it was quieter than ever. I felt I was disturbing an ineffable peace.

I was still wearing my bridal gown—the one I wore in the oracle pit as god's bride. And I noticed that Father looked at it in wonder, though he said nothing.

Mother was lying with a perfectly white face and closed eyes; I thought she was already dead. But when

I sat down beside her and began sobbing she opened her eyes and looked at me with a look I shall never forget. It came from so far away that I don't know how it reached me—reached anything so alien and remote. Who was this unknown woman who had come and sat down at her side, so strangely dressed—dressed for something—she could not remember what?

Then she seemed to recognize me; she saw who I was and realized that I had come at last. It was she who had asked Father to send for me, I learned afterwards, so that she might see me before she died. But what was I wearing? How strangely I was dressed!

Slowly she stretched out her emaciated hand and fingered my bridal gown, the stuff of it, without comprehension. It must have seemed to her that I was masquerading—as indeed I was. She must have thought so—she who had really been a bride and borne children to a man and loved him and them. She lay picking at my fine bridal dress without understanding. With a weary, pained look she closed her eyes and her hand dropped, gaunt and empty.

I left my place at her side and Father took it. With his hand in hers she slipped quietly away.

To my despair I still felt fever and excitement as she went.

With his great coarse hand Father stroked her face, which he had caressed when it was young, and he must have been thinking of much that I had never known and would never hear about—things that belong to the life of mankind.

Unnoticed by him I went and took off my bridal gown and put on an old kirtle which I found somewhere, left over from my youth.

When I came back he was still sitting and looking at her, and he still did not notice me. He saw nothing but her worn face which he had loved when it was alive and loved still—a face as pure and simple as her soul had always been. Now the soul had left it, but it was still filled with the memory of that soul.

I, too, went forward and looked at it, and saw how beautiful and how transfigured it was. But when I saw its infinite peace I wept.

It was we two who had once been so much alike.

He had folded her hands upon her breast, and they were white and thin, almost transparent, though they had toiled at many tasks throughout a long life. Now they were quite white, as if all that was earthly were already being erased from them.

Later we helped each other to wash the dead body and anoint it with oil. Then we carried it to a bier that Father had made and laid it there upon a bed of thyme and olive twigs according to the old custom, to give it back to life. And although I would have helped him, it was Father who with his stiff fingers wove a myrtle wreath and set it about her head, because she was now initiated and a partaker of the divine. He was scrupulous that all things should be duly observed, and so they were.

Finally he laid a few ears of grain upon her sunken breast and covered her face with a cloth, that she might be at peace.

Next day he dug a grave in the grove some little way from the house, not far from the turf altar at which he offered gifts almost every day. Together we carried out the bier, which was heavy for me, for she was not a slight woman, and lowered it into the earth.

Then she lay on her bed of fresh leaves, restored to the earth, to the womb. For the last time we beheld her peaceful face; then Father cast earth upon her and later sowed grain upon the grave, as the custom was. For she belonged not to death but to life.

I stayed with Father for a time to help him settle down. I was able to do this, for the great festival was over. The house needed a woman to look after it, and Father was used to having one. And I was glad to stay there, at least for a time; to walk in the peace and still-ness that reigned there, of which I myself stood in such need. For I was distressed by what had happened —by her fingering my bridal gown and scarcely recog-nizing me—distressed because I had come too late to beg her forgiveness for being no longer like her, be-cause I had disturbed the stillness of her death and be-cause her hand had dropped empty from my lap. Dis-tressed by all these things.

It is strange that the peace in someone's face can be

felt as a reproach, but I did feel it so. I reproached myself for not possessing it, for being incapable of it. I reproached myself for my whole soul, my life, my existence as it had now become. Why was I not like her? Why was my life not like hers? Why was not all life, all the world, like her? Why was not everything as it had been in my childhood? As it was when we used to go down together to the sacred spring in the valley —the one with the ever fresh greenery about its clear waters, and the grains of sand so gently stirred by the invisible finger of god? Why did we not still walk side by side, as then? There was so much I should have liked to talk to her about.

She had lain here waiting for me, but I had not come—until it was too late. I had been too greatly preoccupied with the great festival to think of her, to come down here and find out for myself that she was ill—that she was dying. Too much taken up with things she could not understand—things one could not explain to her. Things that lay beyond her grasp, but held me captive, so that I could not live without them.

Not live without them? But her world—could I live without that? Could I, really?

The great festival which I could not leave—from which I could not tear myself away—the wildness, the rapture, the obsession—what was that compared to the peace in a human face, and to the possession of that peace?

What did I possess? And what had I lost? What was my world to hers—to the world I lost when I forsook her?

I would have sat here at her side in the stillness, holding her hand in mine. It was here I ought to have been.

I perceived that the solemn festival had been here, when my mother lay dying.

Yes, I felt I wanted to stay here for a time and live in this peace and safety. In her world. For a time at least.

Often I sat by the hearth in the place where she used to sit, and I found I liked the smell of the old house. This was strange, for before when I came to see them I never liked it. It had seemed to me unpleasant, probably because I knew it so well. And the quietness, the safety of the place had oppressed me. Now I sank into it, feeling it take me to itself and enfold me. It was sweet to me now.

So it was that I came once more to experience the home of my childhood. To relive the fields, the earth, the old olive tree by the gable end, the grove with its turf altar where Mother now lay, and the path winding down the valley to the spring. All these familiar things became dear to me again; they enfolded me faithfully, and it almost seemed as if I had never left them. Yet I still felt uncertain of their reality, and sometimes I was disturbed by other thoughts; nevertheless it did seem that I was on my way back to real, everyday life.

Father continued his work in the fields and I kept house as best I could. I had lost touch with it and forgotten it, but I soon got into the way of it again. We lived a pleasant life together.

Strangely enough we never talked much about Mother, though we both thought of her constantly. Father erected a stele over her grave and made frequent sacrifice there. They were simple offerings, such as suited them both. I used to see him standing there, and afterwards when he came up to me by the house his gaze was abstracted, as if he were still far away. It was almost odd to see that gentle, sad look in the face of so big and sturdy a man. His gaze was as clear as a child's, though the expression was not at all that of a child. He grew more and more silent, but his melancholy was full of goodness.

I remember him so well as he was during this time —the last I was together with him. He would come slowly in at the door in the evenings, and when he had eaten, his big old hands remained resting on the table, stiff and tired, unused to idleness. Seeing them I could not help recalling how safe and comforting it had felt when in my childhood he held my little hand in his. But now they had greatly altered, and grown old and wrinkled.

Each morning he went down to the solitary tree as

he had always done, the one he worshipped; and then he began the day's work. This was in the early morning light before the sun had risen; for it rises late among these high mountains, though the sky is bright long before.

A little later I took the path to the spring down in the valley, the sacred spring. It was so restful and peaceful to stand there and look into it; it filled me with devotion, and I returned calm, strengthened and, in my own way, happy.

So our life flowed by. Spring came; the country around our place was beautiful, and so was all that mighty valley.

One morning as I was walking down the path I saw a man bending over the spring and drinking from his hand. I remember that while I was still some distance away I noticed that he drank from his left hand. His back was turned to me, yet I saw that this was someone I didn't know, and I slackened my pace, thinking to wait a little before going on. But he had heard me and looked up. He was quite young, a good ten years younger than I was; his face was fresh and frank and deeply browned by the sun. When I looked at it more closely there seemed something familiar about it. And he, too, seemed to know me. He rose, and when I came up to him I found that like me he was from this valley and that I'd seen him sometimes as a child, though that was long ago. He was now a man of twenty-five or thirty, not very tall but broad and powerful and full of health. But he had only one arm.

He recognized me, too, although it was many years since he had seen me. Our homes were not far apart. His parents, like mine, leased a small piece of land from the temple; they were poor people—perhaps even poorer than we, for they had many children.

We chatted together. He told me he had been away for some years as a soldier, having set forth when he was little more than half grown because there were so many of them at home. Then he had lost an arm in the war, and that was why he had come back. He was no good at war now, he said smiling, and it didn't matter. He hadn't liked it, but a man had to do something. The best work of all was tilling the soil, if one had any. But for that, too, one really needed two arms.

Then he asked about me and I told him that Mother had died and that I now kept house for Father.

"Aren't you married then?" he asked.

"No," I answered, hesitating a little.

Then we talked about the spring. I told him how I went to it every morning because my mother had taught me to, and because it was very holy. Yes, he knew that, he said, and the water was sweet. Not even the Castalian spring was so good, and such crowds went there that one couldn't get near it. He had longed for this water all the years he was away. He had returned the evening before and come down here first thing this morning to taste it.

And he knelt down and drank again as if he could never have enough.

"Won't you drink?" he said.

I hesitated and then knelt beside him and we both drank the cold, clear water from our hands. There was nothing extraordinary about this, and yet I felt that it was a singular act we were performing together. Afterwards our faces were reflected side by side in the water, which soon lay still again. I don't know whether he saw how the grains of sand in one corner were being slowly stirred round and round. Perhaps not, but he said, "Nowhere else in the world can there be such glorious water as this. It must, indeed, be a holy spring."

We rose and parted. He was going to wander about the countryside, he said, and see if he remembered it. And with a little smile on his sunburned face he left me and went his way down the valley.

I took the path home, slowly and without turning around, though now and then I wondered which way he was going.

Didn't he know that I was a pythia? Perhaps not?

Next morning I went down there as usual. I lingered perhaps a little longer than usual. He came at last, and I found that I was glad of his coming. It was a strange thing to notice, to feel.

We talked again. He said that yesterday he had been right down to the river at the very bottom of the valley, and had enjoyed going there again. He was astonished to hear that I had never been there. I ought to go, he said; it was not far and not terribly steep if one knew the right places. We might go there together some time, he added, as if it were something quite natural.

When he had drunk from the spring we sat down beside it and he told me of his soldiering life in countries unknown to me. He thought it was fine to be home again, but he did not care for Delphi. It was a city of rogues, and all the women were venal.

"But it has a glorious temple," I said.

"Yes, of course," he answered. But that was all he said. I couldn't make out whether or not he knew that I was a pythia. And anyhow, what did it matter—why was I so curious about it?

If he didn't know now, he soon would.

We talked together as if we'd known each other a long time and were old friends. But now and then we looked at each other not knowing what to say nor quite what it was we had been talking about.

The sun was some way above the mountain when we parted and I went home.

On the third morning—for I remember I counted them, though only half consciously—on the third morning I got ready as soon as Father had gone out to work, and I remember thinking how queer it was to feel my heart beating while I did so. As I came down the path I soon saw that he was already sitting there at the usual place, and I felt suddenly very happy as I walked along through the morning light, which was not yet real light but would soon become so—would soon blossom out in full sunshine over all the valley. He heard me while I was still a long way off, and turned and sat smiling at me as I drew near. And when I reached him and drank from the spring he knelt down at my side, though he had drunk already, and drank again from his hand, which was sun-browned and broad and the back of it very hairy. When he had finished we remained on our knees looking at each other, and all at once without a word he put his hand behind my head and drew it to him and kissed me. Our lips were cold from the chilly spring water but grew gradually warmer—they grew warmer and warmer and at last they were burning hot. I felt his broad wet hand at the back of my neck and I heard myself panting and my heart thudding within me. And when at last his lips left mine I heard him saying in his calm voice, but as if at a distance, "Why do you shut your eyes?"

I had not known as I was doing it. I opened my eyes and saw his smiling, sunburned face close to mine—saw it come nearer again until I saw it no longer but only felt his strong lips on mine, which were parted and waiting for them.

Afterwards we did not speak but only held each

other's hand. It was the first time I had held his hand in mine—his beloved hand which I so well remember even now.

We were both breathing hard when we got up and stood side by side.

"Shall we go down to the river together?" he said gravely. "You've never been there."

I just pressed his hand and looked at him. For it no longer seemed at all strange that he should ask me and that we should go there together.

We sped downhill and presently when the slope steepened he found a place not too difficult for me, though it was not easy either at the rate we were going, and with me so new to it. But at the worst places he helped me, took my body and held me until I regained my footing on the rocky slopes, where roots of stone pines ran everywhere. The ground became wilder and more precipitous, and from below rose the murmur of the river, growing louder and louder until it rushed and thundered. The valley bottom narrowed, it grew as narrow and shut in as a crevasse, and the daylight withdrew until at last it was no more than twilight, filled with the stunning thunder of the torrent. The pines hid the river from us, but we should soon see it. But when at last, breathless and hot with exertion we reached it, we quite forgot this river that we had come to see—we never looked at it—we saw only each other, thought of nothing but ourselves and of sinking into each other's embrace down there in the darkness where none could see us, where all that was done was done in secret. And we sank upon the ground, and with my eyes closed I felt him tear the clothes off me and come into me.

For the first time I experienced love—the marvel of not being alone, of another person being in me. The marvel of embracing another and being myself embraced, and of feeling a profound, wild satisfaction in my powerful body which, without always knowing it, had always longed for this.

Meanwhile I heard the roar of the river about me, smelled the fragrance of the soft carpet of pine needles on which I lay, and which those good trees for untold years, untold summers, had been preparing for me. I would always associate this scent of pine needles and this dull roar with love as it was for me.

I did not want to open my eyes and I had no need to, knowing that my beloved was with me, that my happy body rested limply with him, in his strong arm, which was hard—so comforting and sweet to rest in. And I felt his hand, his left hand stroke my face; it was queer to feel it, but I loved to feel it, and I had never been caressed before by any hands at all, and never would be caressed by any other one than this, than his.

This was human happiness, this was what it was to be a human being. I was as happy as such beings can be. I was just like one of them.

When at last we had had our fill of each other we

climbed up again toward the daylight, toward the sunlight, toward the full, radiant sunshine that now reigned over the whole valley. By the spring, which lay there as still as if nothing had happened, we parted from one another and, happy, I went home.

When I reached the doorpost of the house I grasped it with my still hot hand, and stood leaning against it for a little while, full of my happiness.

Later when I was preparing the meal for Father to eat when he came in from the fields, I began to think it had been very wrong of us to forget the river, and not even to look at it. Perhaps it was angered because of that—because we had not prayed beside it and purified ourselves in it before abandoning ourselves to our love. Because we had thought only of ourselves. Perhaps this was an offense for which we should be punished. There is no river which is not divine; this one by its mighty roar showed us that it was, and perhaps it was angry with us. I could still hear its menacing thunder, it seemed to me, and now in my solitude it frightened me.

Rivers do not easily forgive, as we all know. And god . . .

God? God? Would he forgive me this that I had done?

I belonged to him; I was his bride.

Yes, truly. But I was human, too. I was a human being, a woman like all other women. This was what I had felt and experienced with such unutterable joy.

A joy and a happiness which I had never dreamed of. Which had been stolen from me—by whom?

I was chosen by god; I was god's elect. But I was also chosen by the life of this earth, by ordinary human life, to live it. I was chosen by love, by a man who loved me, who wanted to possess me and whom I wanted to possess. I was his bride. God's bride—and his.

No, I didn't want to think of this. I wanted to think only of how happy I was. Of that alone. Of nothing but that.

But it was god himself who had given me these disturbing thoughts, which I now thrust from me. And he would return with them and never leave me in peace. I didn't know that then. I never dreamed how much reason I had to be troubled on my own account and on my beloved's—I never dreamed what was awaiting us, menacing us.

We knew not what we did when we hurried down into the gorge, to the rushing river.

I tried to immerse myself in my tasks and think of nothing else. But they needed no thought—my hands performed them without my mind. My hands which but now had caressed . . .

To hold his head between them was most wonderful. What was as precious as the head of the beloved, to kiss his lips warm—hot—and see his gaze plunge into mine . . .

I wonder what my own eyes were like as he looked

into them. . . . They must have been like those of one drowning. . . .

If it was found out, what would happen? What frightful thing would happen to us both? But it had been done in secret and no one knew of it. That is, the river knew. And god knew. God knew!

And it would happen again. It would happen again and again; my body cried out for it and would never stifle its cry; my mouth longed to shout it out across the mountains, over all mountains. . . . What would come of it? I feared nothing! Love fears nothing. My only dread was that my beloved—that my beloved might . . .

Did he know? Did he know that I was a pythia, the priestess and bride of god? And if he came to hear of it, would he, like everyone else—would he then . . .

No, I would think of nothing but my happiness. My present happiness, my happiness now, this day. I would think of myself down there among the kindly trees, on their carpet of fragrant needles, resting among them on his arm, his hard arm that was so safe to rest in. . . . Yes, with him there was safety, safety at last. . . . If only god would let me keep it—he who could never be safety. No, he could not; one had to understand that, and I understood. But to a mortal, to one who was no more than human, safety might surely be vouchsafed; two lovers might surely find it in each other's embrace. I, too, might find it at last in my beloved's embrace, I who had longed for it so much . . .

I prayed to god, I remember—prayed that he would let me be happy and find peace in love, in the earthly love that now filled me.

I did not know, I never dreamed that what I prayed for in my innermost heart was something he could never think of granting, something out of all reason: for him to give me up.

Our happiness must have blinded me to the unreasonableness of my prayer and to the impossibility of its being heard. We dwelled blindly in our love, abandoning ourselves to it with only faint misgivings. I alone was troubled at times; my beloved never. It was not in his nature. He belonged to reality, to the earth, to real life, and he feared nothing beyond. That he as well as I had reason to do so never crossed his mind.

No, happily we knew nothing, nothing at all.

We loved each other, sought each other as often as we could, whenever we had the chance. Secretly, for so it had to be—but that only increased our ardor. We loved each other wherever we happened to be, but always in the open, like the animals, like all nature. We were constrained to do this, but we wanted it too; it suited us as we were and as our love was: homeless and happy. Never indoors like other people, but out in the wind and rain and sun. When desire came upon us I remember that we would hide in a cornfield to possess one another, and lie there unseen with our love. Only the eagles hovering high above the valley saw us. I remember once that summer that the grain bloomed and smoked above us as we became one in the sunshine; I remember the smell of the corn and how the air quivered about us in the summer heat.

But never again would I go down to the river. Sometimes he thought we should, for there we would be most hidden. And he wondered why I didn't want to. But I never told him.

I had had enough of that roar, that distant but menacing din which was forever linked with my love. I could never experience love without hearing that sound. Even up in the daylight—yes, in the midst of our happiness in the cornfield—I seemed to hear the muffled roar of the river around me. Or perhaps within me?

I kept my troubled thoughts to myself, and he knew nothing of them. They came upon me mostly when I was working in the house alone, with plenty of time for every kind of thought. Then I would be filled with a dull unease, a vague dread of what the future might have in its womb. Its womb? Once, I remember, when I was looking for something—something quite different—I came upon my bridal gown. I hid it away quickly. Afterwards I walked about that lonely house in a ferment, full of flying thoughts.

If only I could talk to him—to my beloved—about what was weighing on my mind, how much easier it would be. If I could share it with him. Often I thought of confiding in him—asking him if he knew—

if he knew who I was. But I dared not. My love was all too precious to me and I could not bear to lose it. I possessed it now, but if I opened my heart to my beloved, might I not lose him? It had happened to many. If I told him who I was . . .

But he must surely know it already; he could not but know it. So then I might just as well . . .

In the end I did tell him.

And it turned out that he knew I had been priestess of the oracle when he was a child, and perhaps still when he left home as a young boy, but he thought I had given it up long ago, after only a few years, as others did. He was astonished that I was still a pythia —that I was one now. Since his return he had not wanted to talk to anyone about me, so as not to betray our secret, and therefore he had heard nothing. No more than what I myself had told him: that I kept house for my father. I saw that he did not quite know what it meant to be priestess of the oracle, or what it involved. He had been absent from Delphi for so long, and anyway he had never cared about such things—he never troubled his head about them, he said. But he could not conceal his amazement that I was still there—that I was so deeply bound to god. He said nothing outright, but I saw that it made him thoughtful.

I felt relieved that he should take it like this. I was not to lose him, then. He attached little importance to my being a pythia; he was the first person not to regard me as something queer, and avoid me because of it. He had known it all the time—though not that I was a pythia still. He had known, yet loved me so much! What better proof could there be of how little it mattered to him!

Had I not reason to be thankful and happy? I had told him everything and he had understood me and my uneasiness. Yes, though I had said nothing about uneasiness, in so many words. And now I was uneasy no longer. He had understood it all, as a lover does.

I stroked his hand, which was so dear to me, and at last I remember that I kissed it. We parted with many kisses and smiles, as we always did.

Next time we were together, everything was as before. I believe that never, since the very first time, had I embraced him with such passion; my love for him was ardent and thankful as never before and I wanted to show it, to give it him, to give him me, me —all that a woman in love can give with her body, her devotion, her desire. And he received it and gave himself again. But perhaps he was a little surprised at my vehemence. He caressed me afterwards very gently, I remember, almost as if he wanted to calm me.

We didn't talk about it this time; we both avoided it. And we hardly ever spoke of it again. I noticed a certain unwillingness in him to touch on the subject; nor did I want to now that I had confided in him and all was well.

Yes, everything was as before, except that my love

was even hotter now and meant even more to me. I could not help showing how infinitely much it meant to me, how I clung to it, how overmastering was my need of it. Perhaps I showed it all too plainly.

His love was steadier, calmer, like everything else about him; that was why I loved him so. He loved me in his calm, strong fashion and would certainly never fail me; but the violence of my passion seemed not to increase his love for me, and his desire. Indeed it sometimes appeared to make him a little shy of me — just as he seemed shy of recalling what I had told him of myself: who I was, and that I really belonged to god. He seemed almost to withdraw a little from me; and because I thought I detected this, he became more necessary than ever. I clung to him yet more ardently, more breathlessly — I would never let him go! And although I was no longer afraid of losing him — for I wasn't at all — I clung to him as if I thought I might, as if I had something to fear. I had nothing at all to fear, and yet I went on doing it; I rubbed oil into my face, quite needlessly, to soften my skin and take away my wrinkles, though I had none. Although I looked fresh and not at all old — no older than he — nevertheless I did it. And when one morning he was not at the spring I was frantic with despair. Shamelessly I betrayed my insatiable desire for him, showing him how blatantly, brazenly I loved him; and when I did so my eyes must indeed have been like those of one drowning, but I no longer cared—I let him look into them. I hid nothing. Did not wish to hide anything.

My passion was like a savage chasm that sought to engulf him. And I saw that it frightened him.

Yes, my love was too great. Too much love cloys the beloved, but that I didn't know or understand. If I had known, it would have made no difference. For who can determine the degree of loving?

He recoiled before this excess, this wild conflagration that was so foreign to him and his world—to the security and reality in which he lived. It was this very safety that I loved—and loved it so inordinately that I lost it—so ardently that I was bound to lose it. No, my love was of the wrong kind; it did not belong there. In spite of everything I did not belong to this world, the real world of men; I was not meant for it.

His embrace was safety, and was sweet to rest in. But I was not meant for safety. I became a stranger in it, for I loved it far too much.

But he did not cast me off. He was as good to me as before, and we used to have long talks together, sitting hand in hand. When I pressed myself against him and he knew I longed for him I could see that he would rather have drawn back and that I aroused in him no real desire; yet at times he did as I wished and endured my violence and ardor which he could no longer share. That he did this out of kindness was the bitterest thing of all. Bitter, too, to be forced to acknowledge in one's heart how little love has to do with kindness.

Yes, he was very good to me, and it was strange to feel how gently his strong hand could caress and how love died away in it as it did so.

Thus it was between us when the fatal thing happened: when the message came summoning me to the temple. The oracle was to be opened again; a long line of feast days and great crowds of pilgrims awaited me. ·On that last evening I was in despair and could not hide it. He asked me the reason several times but I would not tell him—could not bring myself to tell him. I parted from him in tears, utterly distraught.

Next morning I took out my bridal gown and without a word to my father I stole up the path toward Delphi. It was still dark and I shivered under the cold stars. I did not love god. I loved someone else. But he did not care about me. I was quite alone.

Down in the holy of holies I felt his presence—the presence of him I had betrayed. His breath came roughly to meet me, drugging me; he seemed to snatch at me. The cave was full of him, of his spirit, and the air was heavy and stifling to breathe. The little venomous oracle snakes were out already, darting their cloven tongues after me, and from the cleft that ran to the realms of death the poisonous, sickly fumes rose up to me, and before I was seated on the tripod I felt almost stunned by them. Never have I come so swiftly into his power, to be wiped out and made his alone; it was as if he had been waiting to hurl himself upon me. He seized me by the throat as if to strangle me—squeezed it tight—and horrible hissing noises were forced out through it. It was sheer horror and terror, without respite or delight; never have I known such anguish, never had he treated me so savagely, with such utter fury; but never had he brought me to such a pitch of frenzied ecstasy. They said afterwards that my body had been hurled back and forth and that my shrieks had been heard right out in the temple. It was appalling. But what frightened me most was that in the middle of it all, through it all, from far, far away, I seemed to hear the muffled roar of the river. Was it true? Did I really hear it? And why should it have filled me with such terror?

Afterwards as I lay recovering in the house of the old woman who had care of me, and resting from my dreadful exhaustion, the little oracle servant came and sat beside me. He had felt uneasy about me and wanted to see how I was. He said he had never seen my face so terrifying as it was this time. The priests had thought the same, and talked about it among themselves. They were much pleased with me—with this violent possession by god. But he added cautiously that perhaps I need not give myself so completely to god—that god could not require it of me. A faint smile must have appeared on my weary face as

I listened with closed eyes to his solicitous words, though he never noticed it.

He spoke of god. Of his god. Why did I smile at that?

Then I heard him mention an unknown man who had come rushing down the stairs from the pilgrims' hall into the holy of holies, and had stared at me with horror-stricken eyes. It could not have been anyone from Delphi, for no one from these parts would have attempted anything so mad, so strictly forbidden. The priests of the oracle had been outraged; he was driven forth at once and handed over to the temple guard. No one knew what his punishment would be; perhaps they would just let him go.

It was a strange incident, to be sure, but I hardly heard what he was saying—until he mentioned that he thought the man had only one arm.

I sat up abruptly, and my manner must have been very strange, for the little servant looked at me in astonishment. He couldn't make out why I was suddenly so changed. But seeing that I was not going to lie and rest any longer, he was satisfied that there was nothing seriously wrong with me. He need not be anxious. Smiling all over his friendly face he left me.

I remained alone with my conflicting thoughts. Why had he come? I did not understand. What reason had he? Could it mean that somehow he—that he cared about me?

Something like a faint hope began to stir in me, though there were no grounds for it.

Slowly I took off the bridal robe, put on my ordinary clothes and set off down to the valley.

I found the house empty and went out again, to stray at random through the fields. Then I saw him at work on a piece of land cultivated by his father, and went over to him. He started a little when he caught sight of me, and I noticed something shy in his look, which as a rule was the most candid look one could meet. His eyes would not meet mine when I came up to him. We both stood silent.

I understood. He had seen me—seen the horror that was my face when I belonged to god—seen what no one can endure to see and what no one can ever forget once he has beheld it. For him I was now the pythia, the possessed; for him as for everyone else. Now he was like everyone else. Now everything was over.

I asked him, and he answered frankly that it was so. He would never get over it. And I understood that what he meant was that no man could love a woman whom he had seen thus, whom he had seen possessed by god.

Then he told me that he had come to the spring that morning and waited for me. When I didn't appear he grew anxious, remembering how strangely distraught I had been the evening before; and he began to think that something must have happened to me. He went up to our house and found it empty, and even more agitated he sought out my father in the fields; but Father didn't know where I was, either, and was surprised to hear that I wasn't at home. Hesitating and reluctant, as if it were something he would rather not speak of, he admitted that I might be up in Delphi, at the temple of the oracle. Hearing this he hurried up there, and while still in the entrance hall he had heard my wild shrieks as if people were hurting me; he dashed through the temple into the pilgrims' hall whence the cries seemed to be coming, and down the stairs . . . And here he broke off.

I took his hand.

"Were you so anxious about me?"

"Yes."

"You needn't be, any more. Never again. I will show you how much I love you."

He understood what I meant: that I would now do for him the utmost and last that any lover can do: release him, so that he would never need to see me again. We would part now; he should live in his world and I in mine, as we ought always to have done.

We stood for a long time looking at the ground and avoiding each other's eyes. And I held his hand, but not tightly enough to remind him of how much I loved him or how hard a struggle I was having now. And so we parted forever.

Although we lived quite near to each other, we

never met again; it was clear that he was avoiding me, thinking it best for us both. I thought so, too, and was grateful to him.

Whenever I did not have to be up at Delphi I lived as before with my father amid the same scenery, in the same valley as the man from whom I had parted. It was late summer now, and everything seemed scorched—the whole of that mighty landscape seemed scorched—fields, woods and all. Only the spring was changeless, as full as ever of its limpid water, because it was divine. The grains of sand in one place were still stirred by an invisible finger. I still went down to it in the mornings as I used to do, and sat there for a little alone with my thoughts. But I never mirrored my face in it. I never wanted to see my face again. I just sat there gazing out into empty space, which was growing paler and more autumnal. And when with closed eyes I had drunk of the water a few times I turned home again.

He must surely have gone there every day, too, for like me he loved that fresh water and could not do without it. But he came at another time of day, when he knew I would not be there. He could trust me not to be there then.

But once I spied him at a distance, gathering olives in a little grove that belonged to his father's holding. I recognized him from the difficulty he was having in keeping the branch still while he plucked the olives. Unknown to him I stood watching him for a long time as he stretched his one arm up into the old tree and gathered its fruit. I could not see his face, but I recognized him. At last I sank down upon the ground and lay there weeping, weeping.

When I came home I sat down with my face in my hands, to think about him; for I was alone. If only I could have helped him hold the branch while he picked! If I could have lived with him on earth, here in the valley, a long and happy human life. As Mother had lived; as so many, many others had been allowed to live. Why couldn't I? Why couldn't I be like the rest?

That was the last time I saw him, though I didn't know it then.

Not long afterwards it happened that I was carried out of the oracle pit unconscious, violated by god. No one knew this; they knew only that he had filled me as never before; that my ecstasy, my frenzy was measureless and that I should have fallen from the tripod had not the little oracle servant noticed it and caught me in his arms.

What happened was just as I was losing consciousness I smelled a sour stench of goat; and the god in the shape of the black goat, his sacred beast in the cave of the oracle, threw itself upon me and assuaged itself and me in a love act in which pain, evil and voluptuousness were mingled in a way that revolted me. How could I feel delight? But I did, I did, though afterwards it filled me with revulsion and self-disgust.

Was it because I had lost my beloved, and had been forsaken by him forever, and because my yearning for him was boundless? Was that the reason? But with loathing I felt that not he but a stranger possessed me, mastered me—a wild and terrible power which stunned me with its ruthless enormity. And simultaneously with this power there was also somehow the he-goat of the oracle pit, with its vile stench. While it was going on I heard the mighty roar of the river as never before; it mounted and mounted, grew more violent and filled me in the midst of my lusting with a pain and terror beyond compare.

Then I swooned right away, and knew nothing more until I woke up in the house of the old woman, who slunk about me with ingratiating malice in her inquisitive, observant eyes. I begged her to leave me alone, and at last, reluctantly and suspiciously, she did so. I could think and suffer my torment in peace. I lay there for a long time, and had not the strength to set off home before the evening.

Did it happen at the same time? It's impossible to say. It was next day that they found him drowned and shattered in the river, but it must have happened the day before, for it was then he left home, in the morning—the morning this ordeal of mine took place. How it had come about no one knew, nor what he was doing down there. He had no reason to go down into that dark gorge. They did not know that he had a reason—that he had been summoned there to his destruction—that he had been drawn there by an invisible power which sought to destroy him, to devour him. Had he been drowned, or had he perished in the rapids from his injuries? Perhaps he had been struck senseless and then died in the river, though there was less water in it now. Had he lain there unconscious, like me, at its mercy? Who knew? They found him lying outstretched on his back, just beneath the surface, fully visible when they came to look for him.

That he had fallen was evident, for in his one hand he still clutched a twig which they supposed he had grasped to save himself. But the strange thing was that it was a twig of the god's own tree, though no laurels grew in that narrow cleft. It seemed to them odd, but they thought no more about it, knowing nothing of what had really happened—of its true meaning. They did not know that it was god's vengeance on human happiness and on his elect, who had betrayed him and had not been willing to live for him alone.

Those who found him said he lay as if sleeping, but bereft of color, bleached—he who had had all the fresh colors of health. His body was covered with bloodless wounds. All the blood had been carried away by the river. It was the river that had taken him. It had taken everything.

I never saw him myself; how could I? Many others saw him, for his strange death attracted a good deal of attention. Many saw him who had no interest in

him, save for the singular manner of his death. But not
I. My love prevented me, for it might have betrayed
itself and become known. I could not go to his home,
to which they had carried him, lest I should arouse
surprise and perhaps suspicion in his parents; I barely
knew them. I could do nothing. Nothing but weep in
solitude, when Father could not see me. He never
noticed that I had wept, he never suspected anything.
He never had, throughout the time our love had
lasted. But it was from him I learned of my beloved's
death and of how they had found him—learned what
everyone else knew, for everyone in the valley was
talking about it.

Soon it was forgotten. He was not well known in
his native place, having been so long away from it.
He had never worked there or been in company with
the others. And now he was dead. He would never
own any land of his own to cultivate with his one arm,
as he had so longed to do.

But I did not forget him. I mourned him until I
seemed torn to tatters, and as if through his death I
had lost life itself, although by that time he didn't
belong to me at all—I had lost him before then, and
lost my life when his love died. I was losing nothing
now. But I couldn't help thinking of him who had
given me everything and then taken everything away—
who in his boundless goodness had allowed me to live.

I have never forgotten him, and I never shall, although it's all so long ago—although it's so far away

that one might think I would see it only through a haze. But I see him before me as alive as if he had never had to die.

How strange it is to sit here and remember him again, and remember the only real life I ever lived.

It was a hard time for me. And it was hard to hide my sorrow. No one must be allowed to guess that anything had happened to plunge me into despair. But because I had the lifelong habit of dissembling, shutting myself in, I think I succeeded and that no one noticed anything. No one but the old woman up in Delphi. She had a wide knowledge of human nature because she so disliked people and everything to do with them; it sharpened her eyes and nothing escaped her.

Sometime in late autumn my monthly flow failed to appear, and I began to be haunted by the thought that I might be with child. It filled me with dread and with a wonderful, budding joy. What this would do to my life—if I lived at all—I had no idea. But in my heart I felt a joy which was quite independent of this. I was filled with an exaltation so soft that no ear could hear it—no one outside myself could have heard it—which whispered of a marvel—whispered softly but persistently, ceaselessly, of something unheard-of: a triumph over death itself. Over the death of love and over death itself. I had to sit quite motionless with closed eyes to take it in, to sense my body's quiet rejoicing at its victory. But I heard, ah I heard it clearly! My love was not dead, it lived on within me! My beloved was not dead, he was within me once more! He had not forsaken me, would never forsake me; never again.

My love had conquered at last. And I had won him back.

It was a happiness so great that it was impossible to see how I could go about among people without their suspecting it—that I could keep such a thing secret. But the very fact that it was my own well-guarded secret—that it was going on inside me without anyone guessing at it—only made my happiness greater and more wonderful, and the miracle rarer.

I was afraid, certainly. Sometimes I thought of what lay before me with anxiety, even terror. But I did not quite know how it would be—I could not picture it—it was half-unreal, for in a sense there was no future for me any more. I was without a future, and thereby marvelously free and released from fear. How could I fear anything in my present condition—the condition we call blessed? My quiet, inward jubilation drowned every other sound—all dread, all fear, all terror—and turned my peril into something scarcely real. I lived only in the reality which I bore within me. For me, that was all there was.

Winter came, and with it my pregnancy advanced like spring, like early summer, carefree, though all nature seemed dead; free from any kind of care. No one noticed, for so far there was nothing to see. Although so great a miracle was coming to pass, no one could see what was happening to me.

Where the old woman was concerned, however, I was not so sure, and I wondered about it more and more. She was as amiable as ever, as amiable as she always was to everyone. But she often looked at me curiously, observing me as only women can observe each other. It was unpleasant and it worried me. But I had always disliked her looking at me, I reminded myself. And she said nothing, gave no hint that she knew or guessed anything. She just looked at me in that curious way.

A time would come when I should realize why her look had always made me feel like that—when I should know that she was always watching me; that it was indeed her duty to do so, though a very congenial duty; that she was to some extent responsible for the pythia and must know all about her and spy on her, on this chosen one who through her close ties with god was so important to the temple and to all Delphi; that she must supervise her conduct and report everything, however trivial, to the priesthood. And this she was more than willing to do.

There was seldom anything to report beyond the usual gossip, in which only she was interested; but now she had something to tell which so far as she knew had never happened before—something which they would listen to at last, with amazement and horror. Something about me, of whom, to her annoyance, she had never before had anything to tell.

When at last she was sure that I was with child she must have wondered how it could have come about. I was as solitary as anyone could be, never seeing a soul, either man or woman, except my old father. To this day I can't make out how she discovered the secret of our love; I thought it belonged to us two alone and could never be touched by the impure thoughts and words of others. But suddenly one day, through her, the priests and the whole city knew of my unspeakable offense against god, against the temple and sacred Delphi; they knew that I was with child and that the father was the man who had been found dead down in the river—who had already had the punishment he deserved—and that this was the same one-armed man who had tried to force his way into the holy of holies and desecrate it, perhaps to rob the god of his property, his priestess, just when she was filled with his spirit.

God had judged him already. But I remained. The guiltier criminal remained. For he had been an ordinary mortal, while I was chosen by the divine, to be used by it for its own purposes and to serve it devotedly, faithfully and with perfect self-abnegation. And the fact that I had done so, and that since first becoming a pythia as a young girl I had lived only for the temple and god, and had been regarded by all as almost part of the oracle; that I was reputed to be so dearly beloved by god that he would speak through no one else, and that this reputation of mine benefited the holy place and with it all Delphi—all this made my guilt the blacker, my fall the deeper, the sudden hatred of me the more savage. That I should have outraged and deceived god, failed him, forsaken him for an earthly man, was an incredible crime, an infamy without parallel.

I was brought before a council of the senior priests, who asked me whether what the old woman said was true. From what they knew of me and from the good opinion they had formed of me as a priestess of the oracle throughout all these years of service in the temple, it seemed to them utterly beyond belief. It was plain that they wanted it not to be true. But I admitted it at once; indeed, it must have been evident that I was glad to be carrying a child, and this amazed and outraged them more than ever. They talked excitedly among themselves about this extraordinary, unheard-of event, and about the harm it would do to the prestige of the oracle; and they said that by rights I ought to be hurled over the cliff, from which desecrators of the temple were usually thrown, though I realized that they were not going to sentence me to that. Then they turned to me and talked about god and the fearful crime I had committed against him, and then more about the dishonor I had brought upon the temple and the oracle and all Delphi. They ended by saying that god required the sternest of punishments to be inflicted upon me, and that this would be decided upon in the course of the day.

Nevertheless it was not they who sentenced me, for through their delay my fate was determined by others.

The rumor that I had confessed and that the tale was true ran through the city like wildfire, and turbulent mobs gathered outside the old woman's house where, as they knew, I was awaiting my sentence. They were armed with sticks and stones, and they yelled that I must die. I could see them through the window; I could see they were the kind to carry out their threats. Their faces were horrible in their insensate hatred, their mob malignity. Inside the house the old woman padded about with ill-concealed gloating in her rat-gray face, pretending to be alarmed on my account and at the same time protesting that she would be responsible for me no longer, that I must go—go out to them, that's to say, so that they could kill me. Never by a sign did she admit that it was she who had informed against me, and I did not care to tell her that I knew; perhaps she thought I didn't. She may even have felt guiltless of my fate—of what was now to befall me—for she always regarded herself not only as a righteous but as a very kind person, who never said a bad word about anyone, though all around her were mean and false and wicked in every way.

The yells and threats grew wilder, and the priests did nothing; they never interfered, but seemed glad to leave my sentence to the mob and escape having to deal with me themselves. My situation there in that house, with the furious, murderous crowd outside and the gray, slinking, poisonous creature in the room behind me was vile and horrible and I felt no hope of ever getting out of it alive.

It was then that my only friend came: the little servant of the oracle. He ran in breathlessly in his slapping sandals and urged me to hide in the temple —to take refuge there, for it was holy ground where no one could do anything to me, for I would be under god's protection. The old woman was indignant at this suggestion—at the mere thought of the sanctuary being used for such a purpose, or of god protecting a lecherous woman like me, a woman who had betrayed him. Little wonder if she was outraged at the idea; she was thinking of the good name of the temple which lay so near her heart; of the sacred place which she felt appointed to guard and which was the apple of her eye, although she hardly ever set foot in it. Was it really to be used in this way, and would I perhaps escape punishment altogether? Never before had I seen any evil in her face—in that dead gray face which I now beheld for the last time —but now she could conceal her nature no longer.

The little oracle servant noticed nothing, however, and dragged me away in an attempt to save my life.

The woman's house stood so close to the temple that it might be possible to slip from one to the other before the mob spied me. The people were massed before the house, but at one end there was a way out which they might have forgotten. We slipped out so quickly that no one saw us; but when we ran up the steps into the temple we were seen, of course, and a wild yelling broke out behind us. The mob rushed after us and in a few moments they had filled the whole stairway. By then we had come through the colonnade and into the temple itself, and I still remember that in spite of the danger and excitement the first thing my friend thought of was to take off his sandals and to see that I did the same; a thing I should certainly have forgotten otherwise. It was so like him—god's little friend and mine—to remember first and foremost that this was a holy place. That was why we were safe. If we really were? The mob seemed to have no veneration for the sacred room; they poured into it screeching and I only just escaped by running further into the interior of the temple. They screamed like lunatics, saying that they would rid god of this scum, this whore of a priestess who had dishonored him and their city.

But all at once the gentle, kindly little oracle servant altered in a way I could not have imagined. In a loud, firm voice which I had never before heard from him, he declared that this was god's holy place, and that whoever dared to force his way into it should die the death, and by the hand of the avenging god himself. Anyone who sought sanctuary in here stood under god's mighty protection.

Didn't they know that? he exclaimed in a fury; and the rabble with all their hot, repulsive faces recoiled before him in fear; for what he said was well known to all and no one could doubt its truth. They moved out again into the colonnade, and because it seemed to him that some were not moving fast enough he angrily seized his broom which was standing by the entry, and swept them out, as if they were the dirt which it was his duty to clear away, since he was appointed by god to keep his sanctuary clean.

Having expelled them all he stayed in the colonnade to make sure they did not try to come in again. He must have succeeded, for no one appeared and it was now almost quiet; I heard no more than a sustained murmur and now and then a single shout.

I was alone in the temple. Alone under god's protection. He had not denied it me, he had not quite forgotten that I was his. He received me into his embrace. And into his radiant embrace, in his temple up in the daylight. In the temple of his glory, where I had never been permitted to serve him. He received me there at last.

It was most strange. In this desperate hour when the mob were waiting outside to assault me, and perhaps take my life, I was filled with stillness and solemnity—now at last he filled me with the serenity of his whole being for which I had so often prayed, but which he had never before vouchsafed me. Now at last I felt the safety for which I had so besought him, now at last he let me rest in his embrace. I knew it would only be for a little while—it could not be for long, for my fate was sealed. Yet I was deeply happy.

I looked about me with the same reverence and joy as when I had stood here with my mother and beheld his dwelling place for the very first time, believing that it was here that I was to serve him. Of course that could not be. But now he received me here in his true sanctuary, and gave me shelter and safety in my hour of mortal danger. And I felt how near he was to me—closer perhaps than ever before—not as heat and fire, but rather as light. I felt his light pouring over my face so that my eyes, which I kept closed for very happiness, were scalded by tears.

Now this cruel, inscrutable god was shedding all his light and all his peace upon me; now, when all was over and I was to leave his temple forever. Now for a while he bestowed upon me his serenity, his safety. For a little time, while hoarse voices shouted for me outside and penetrated the stillness of the temple, came the peace he was giving me at last.

I have never forgotten that hour. Never ceased to be thankful for it. But neither have I ever understood why he is like that; why things need be as they are.

Was it because of this that, having recovered and

summoned up all my strength, I was able to leave the temple, though the mob were still outside watching for me and desiring nothing more than that I should leave my refuge? I don't know what made me do so—perhaps an impulse from god, or on the contrary some inner defiance of him, a self-assertion, a challenge to this ruthless, enigmatic deity. Or perhaps quite simply pride, a contempt for death and for the rabble outside. Whatever it was, I determined to leave my sanctuary and go out to meet my fate, were it life or death. In any case I could not have stayed in the temple forever, and would have had to go in the end.

When the little servant saw me putting on my sandals again he was dismayed, for he guessed what I meant to do. Whispering he tried to dissuade me from anything so mad. But I had made up my mind, and for all his entreaties I would not relent.

To their amazement I stepped into the colonnade and out onto the steps. They were too much astonished to do anything—even to shower abuse upon me—they simply stared and drew back. It was as if when at last I showed myself—when they actually saw me—I terrified them as I had terrified them during my life as a pythia—and more than any other priestess of the oracle, because I was believed to have been specially chosen by god and filled and possessed by him as no one else had ever been. And now, although he had cursed me, they may have thought

that his power remained in me, if only as a frightful
malediction. It frightened them, held them back, and
not one of them dared come near me. I think they
were frightened, too, by the very fact that I dared to
leave the temple and face them of my own free will.
It was past understanding; no ordinary person would
do such a thing; there was something not human in
the act.

They stood ready to hurl themselves upon me—
they had no greater desire—but though hatred
burned in their eyes they kept at a safe distance.

And when I went down the steps and out into the
temple court, to continue down the sacred road, they
made way for me, so that I passed between two lines
of savage people armed with sticks and stones who
dared not molest me. But those who stood furthest
away now began to shout and yell, and soon abuse
was hailing down upon me from all sides: the foulest
names a woman can be given, and even mocking com-
ments upon the age at which I had conceived. They
stopped at nothing in their moral indignation and
their rage over the shame I had brought upon the
city, the temple and god. The blow to their livelihood, the unprecedented disgrace to Delphi and the
oracle, might cause the stream of pilgrims to dwindle
away and with it their income. Their faces were
blood-red with unnatural excitement, and to my dis-
gust I recognized many of them, for they were all
from Delphi; no strangers came here at this time of

year. Men and women jostled one another in this mob of every class and order; and women not least, my own kind, who ought to have understood me better and forgiven me; for what had befallen me had happened through love. My crime, after all, was what they, too, called love.

These loathsome faces might have inspired me with enduring hatred for mankind, had not reflection shown me that this was not the whole truth about them. But just then it was the whole truth, and a dangerous and frightful truth it was.

The mob followed me and ran alongside me, shrieking continued insults and threats. But they never touched me; they dared not. Perhaps this was because I was on the sacred road. That too was hallowed ground where no one might be molested and no deed of violence committed. And perhaps something of the fear put into them by the little servant still remained.

At a bend in the road I turned for a last glimpse of him, my friend, the only person who wished me well; and there he was on the temple steps looking after me, standing with his broom and weeping. It grieved me sorely and I found it hard to keep back my tears. Next moment he was hidden from me, and at once I felt utterly alone.

So I walked along this sacred way, where one morning in my first youth—god's glorious morning—I had passed with such rapture, arrayed as god's bride and full of my love for him. I was walking here now for the very last time, and in how different a manner! Threats and revilings were poured upon me and I did not know what lay before me; yet strangely enough I was quite calm. As calm as I had been in the temple. Though now surely it was my own calmness—something I had fought for and won by myself. Or was it not?

This calmness of mine, in such a situation may also have struck them as unnatural and made them shy of molesting me. I believe this was why they dared not use their sticks on me, their former pythia—why they shunned even that contact with her and with the power that might still be in her. But when the sacred road came to an end—when I had to leave it and try to climb the mountain slopes—there arose such an outcry as was never heard before, and a hail of stones fell all about me. Some hit me, but not so as to endanger my life, and it seemed as if the people were not trying to kill me—as if they dared not—and were content to drive me from the city. But one stone struck the back of my neck so hard that I sank to the ground and could hardly get up again. After a time I did so and continued up the mountain. And they didn't pursue me; they stood shrieking their curses at me and warning me never to set foot in Delphi again.

When I had come away from them and out of sight I sat down and breathed more freely. I was saved. I was bleeding from some wounds, especially the one at the back of my neck; when I put my hand there it was covered with blood, and my body was bruised all over. Apart from that I was whole and had come off lightly, considering the mortal danger I had been in.

What I had dreaded most was that they might so injure me that my child might not reach its full term —that I might be hurt in body or mind in a way fatal to a woman in my condition. But I need not have been anxious, for nothing of the kind had happened. My strong body stood up to this rough treatment, which might have broken many another, and my mind preserved its serenity. If god had had anything to do with this serenity and it was not of my own winning, I was thankful to him for it. It may have helped to save me and through me the child. But could it be supposed that god would want to save the child?

The one to whom I chiefly owed my life was the little servant of the oracle. Had it not been for him I should never have survived this frightful day, I thought, when I looked back that evening at what had happened, and prepared to spend my first night under the open sky. I thought of him still when I had lain down to rest on some leaves I had swept together, in a hollow. From here no human dwelling was to be seen, only the steep mountain sides and between them the stars. In this solitude I found that it did me good to think of him, my only friend.

I had no idea what he really thought about my crime. He helped me, he saved my life, he took my part entirely. But what he thought of the act of which I was guilty and which was the cause of all that had happened I never knew. We never exchanged a word about it; indeed, we never had the chance.

Probably he simply did not understand that I had committed any offense at all. Being incapable of seeing evil in anyone he condemned no one, not even me. It was not in his nature to do so.

But what of his faith in the goodness of mankind? The scenes he had witnessed today, which aroused in him such indignation—how would they affect his trust in everything and everyone about him, in god and in man? Would they bring his vision of the world toppling about his ears?

No, I hoped that he would soon forget it—forget the tumult I had caused in his life, and go on as before, believing the best of everyone, as was natural to him. That was how he ought to be, the little friend of god and man, and that was how I preferred to remember him.

In that hope I fell peacefully asleep.

The cold woke me several times that night, and I was glad when at last the sun came to shed a little warmth. It was the middle of winter, and the nights were really chilly.

Yet I remember that it was a mild winter, and luckily so, for otherwise I could not have survived.

Even as it was, it was bad enough. It was difficult to sustain life—difficult to keep from starving and to endure the cold at night. I sought shelter in holes or in deserted herdsmen's huts, and at first I lived solely on dry, half-rotten old berries which I found in the mountains, and on the seeds from pine cones—anything which gave nourishment or seemed to give it. I roamed far and wide to find these berries, whose name I did not know. Then I grew bolder and more enterprising, driven to it by hunger and the thought of the child: it must live and not be harmed by my starvation. There were goats on the mountain, and I coaxed them to come to me so that I could milk them. I collected the milk in a bowl I had taken from one of the huts and drank it with a desperate greed. I became more daring and adroit at stealing milk in this way, for nothing could have been better for me and the child than this delicious food. I even ventured to creep into inhabited huts and steal the herdsmen's cheese and bread; I used to lie low among bushes and boulders nearby, and creep out when they were gone. In this way I came by a goatskin to spread over me at night. I stole anything and would gladly have committed any crime for the sake of the child, his and my child, the child of our love; the sign that our love was not dead and that it lived on in me; that my beloved was still within me.

I lived like a savage, like a wild animal up there in the mountain. I was forced into it, having been cast out by men from the life of men; and like a tormented, gravid beast I shunned no means of keeping myself and the child alive. I carefully avoided inhabited places and all to do with mankind, for I could expect no good from them. And I was always much afraid that the herdsmen would discover me. They would hurt me, too, for they, too, were men.

Nevertheless I was happy during this time. Happy in my freedom and in my healthy body, which knew that it could live in this way without taking harm, which toiled hard but became the stronger for it and the fitter to endure. And I was happy in the knowledge that it was his child I carried in me and was to bring forth. I felt it, living and stirring in me continually, and it gave me great joy. Despite all hardships, anxieties, cold and hunger, in my loneliness and exile I experienced the measureless happiness of motherhood.

And when at last the spring came everything was easier, or seemed so. I was no longer cold, and soon there would be more for me to eat as for other beasts of the field. I found juicy herbs which tasted fresh and wholesome, though they were not filling, and the goats' milk was richer than before. The goats were not hard to call; they came of their own accord to be milked, perhaps because they knew me now and perhaps because they liked being milked by a woman. Often they followed me and I had to drive them off—chase them right away—for I was afraid that the herdsmen would notice. Even animals that had never seen me before sometimes followed me.

This was the first time I noticed that they were in some way attracted to me, though I saw nothing odd about it at the time and thought it quite natural.

The hills turned bright with flowers of all kinds, and at night I smelt their rich fragrance, sick at heart for him who had loved me and bestowed on me the miracle of spring. The only spring my body ever had.

If he had lived, would he have been with me now —would he have come back to me now that I was no longer a pythia, and because I was carrying his child? Would we have shared this life and been happy in it together?

What vain thoughts! He was dead. He lived no longer and would never live again. They had found him down there in the river, pale and bloodless, bereft of life's color, with a twig of the god's own tree in his hand. Thus it was. Thus it would be forever.

Man's destiny is but one. When it is accomplished nothing remains.

Only the gods have many destinies and need never die. They are filled with everything and experience everything. Everything—except human happiness. That they can never know and therefore they grudge it to men. Nothing makes them so evil and cruel as that men should presume to be happy and forget them for the sake of their earthly happiness. Then they claim their revenge. And put a twig of their tree in their victim's hand.

Now and then on really still nights I thought I could hear the river far below; the river which encompassed our love with its mighty roar and afterwards proved so fatal to us and took so grim a revenge. Now it was spring again; no doubt the waters were running in spate through the narrow gorge, and the sound of them may well have carried as far up as this

For surely I could not have been hearing it only within myself?

No, I distinguished it clearly, coming from the gorge. I lay here among the flowers, quite alone, and heard the river, the cruel river that had carried away the blood of my beloved.

So spring was both a sweet and a sorrowful time for me, as it is for all lovers who are alone. Alone? But I was not alone! How could I say so? In my womb was my beloved still; there our love lived on, conquering death and his own death. Conquering even god himself. It was perhaps presumptuous to say so; nevertheless it was true. God had taken his life in vain, and in vain had swept his blood away down the river. He lived again in me, with new blood which I had given him, my own heart's blood, the blood with which I had loved him, love's human blood of which the gods know nothing.

So it was. So our struggle with god had ended.

And summer came, serene summer, the season of

ripening and fulfillment when nature's womb rejoices. The valley, ringed by its mighty mountains, was a womb full of maturing life, and up here, too, all that could live on these wild slopes lived and throve. All was brightness and ease, calmness and confidence, and I, too, felt secure and confident, though there was much to make me anxious: the birth itself, how I should manage afterwards, how I should feed the child, and much else. If anyone had reason to dread the future it was surely I, but I did not. It was useless to burden myself with that, too. I was confident and carefree, as a woman in my blessed condition should be. My sturdy body grew big and shapeless, yet I moved almost as nimbly as before, because my way of life had been so active and natural throughout. The female animal which must forage for herself while carrying her young brings forth easily, I thought to myself; and I believed that I would do so, too. For I knew nothing about it.

The weather grew hotter and summer seemed so far advanced that I thought my time must soon come. But it didn't. It didn't come and didn't come —nothing happened. I was puzzled. The time must have passed, but by how long I didn't know. I knew when we had been together for the last time—for the very last time. But I would not think of that: it was more than I could bear. . . . I wanted only to remember that I was to bring forth the fruit of our love, I wanted only to live in the memory of that love at its most beautiful: when it was equally strong in both of us, when we so loved each other that we conquered everything. Now I was to bear our child, our love's child, the child of the dead man, of the sacrifice; I was to bring forth our triumph, our victory over death and over all things. Over god himself.

But I did not bring forth. Time passed and passed —and nothing happened.

Summer continued, the heat continued and grew more terrible and oppressive and exhausting; only the nights brought a little coolness sometimes, when a chill came down from the mountains and their eternal snows.

I have never known so hot a summer. In my condition I suffered especially severely from the heat, burdened with my big, heavy body which hitherto had not troubled me. I had swelled out even more now; I felt I could hardly grow any bigger and that the time must have come for me to be delivered. But I was not delivered. It seemed as if I should never bear this child.

But one day as I lay languishing in the heat I felt that the pains were beginning at last. Slight at first, then stronger, and after that more violently and at shorter intervals. The sun scorched down as never before, with stabbing, red-hot rays, and the air felt stiflingly heavy, hardly to be breathed, though that may just have been my own fancy. Suddenly great sulphur-yellow clouds towered up over the horizon in the south and rapidly approached. For the first time that summer a storm seemed to be on the way. Darkness fell over the whole valley, and the menacing, sharp-edged shadow of the storm clouds came nearer and nearer. Suddenly a lightning flash cut through the clouds, visible despite the brightness of the day, followed by the dull rumbling of the thunder.

I had never thought of this, or taken it into account. I had expected to bear my child out in the open, anywhere, but not to need any kind of shelter. Where was I to go? I could not lie out in the pouring rain, exposed perhaps to the lightning, which often struck down here among the mountains.

I rose and looked about me. There was nothing here to give shelter, not so much as a tree, and I wandered off at random across the mountain side, to search. The pains came on again, worse than before, and because of them I had to bend forward as I walked and hold myself hard about the belly. What would be the end of it? Where should I go to have my child?

It was then that the goats came. Goats which I had never seen before and which could not possibly have known me: I believe they were wild ones. But they seemed to understand what was the matter with me, and when I moaned they uttered a whining, pitying cry which had a peculiar, almost human sound. Some of them sprang eagerly up the hillside and down to me again, as if wanting to lead me up there. It wasn't easy for me to follow them uphill, but I did it, rather unsteadily, as if something were urging me on. Sometimes, when the pains beset me too severely, I had to pause, and the beasts seemed to understand, for they halted, too, and waited for me to go on again. At last the climb was almost vertical and I thought I could go no further. But seeing this they bleated so pitifully that I had not the heart to grieve them, and summoning up all my strength I began to climb after them up the steep cliff. This evidently pleased them, and they gave eager bleats of satisfaction.

Behind me I heard the storm approaching; the lashing rain moved up from the valley, closer and closer, the thunder roared over the whole country-side, and the cliff which I was climbing and clinging to with hands and feet glimmered in the ever more frequent flashes of lightning.

At last, utterly exhausted, I reached a small plateau —a little place that was more or less level—and just as the rain beat down upon me I spied an opening in the rock before me, leading right into the hill. The goats were already thronging into it, and dazed and reeling I followed them.

The cave was almost dark, at least until one's eyes became accustomed to it, and even afterwards it was so dim that I could not see how large it really was. But it seemed a fair size and ran on indefinitely into the darkness. A sour goat-smell came to meet me.

Then I knew no more, and sank to the ground, which was covered with a thick layer of old, dry goat droppings. It made a soft bed, and to me it was delight unspeakable to sink down upon it.

I must have been unconscious for a time, for when I came to myself again all the goats were standing around gazing at me with anxious, pitying eyes. My awakening gave rise to lively bleatings. But when immediately afterwards I was assailed by the most appalling pains—pains of a different kind from the earlier ones, I thought—and began screaming wildly, they fell quiet and withdrew a little in alarm; then they came back and began to cry out as I did, uttering strange, plaintive cries which though not as loud as my own were in a way even more sorrowful, like the sighing of cattle: helpless and bestial. Yet these creatures made me feel less alone in my suffering. They shared it, though they could express themselves in no other way—in no human way—and for that matter neither could I. We had the same language and understood one another well.

The pains came now at such short intervals that there seemed hardly any pause between them—just long enough to draw a few breaths—and they were so frightful that the whole cavern resounded to my screams. I could not repress my screaming, and it relieved me a little, too. Some of the goats ran to and fro in agitation, while others stood still around me as before, with outstretched heads, lamenting, though now they could seldom be heard, for my own cries drowned theirs. But I saw their muzzles quiver with their frightened bleating, and their upper lips moved continuously up and down over their moist, yellowish-white teeth.

At the time it never struck me that there was anything strange about the animals' behavior and their preoccupation with me; I had no thought for that or for anything else. But I was thankful that they were there all about me, so that forsaken though I was by god and all mankind I did not have to be quite alone in this hour. They were the only beings who cared about me, or cared that in my agony I was to bring forth a child.

Outside the storm continued, and now it was right over us. Thunderclaps followed close upon one another, the rain fell in sheets before the mouth of the cave, and the cave was repeatedly lit by the flashes of lightning. It was as if the whole sky were on fire and were darting in to us its panting tongues of flame.

The violence of the pains told me that the birth itself had started, and though half swooning I was aware that the baby was beginning to force its way out. A dim notion that it was always worst at the beginning while the head was emerging passed through my mind; otherwise I thought of nothing. I helped as much as I could, or rather my body did so without asking my leave; it labored with a violence I would never have wished or thought myself capable of producing. I felt as if I should be rent in pieces; I was mad with agony, and sometimes only half-conscious, for I heard my screams as if they were someone else's. How long it lasted I have no idea, for I lost all sense of time.

But at last I felt a sudden relief and liberation. There was still pain, certainly, but of quite a different kind; I breathed more calmly and did not have to scream—only moan slightly—and my body did not have to strain; it slackened—everything in me slackened and it was a glorious sensation; it was as if I had returned to life.

When I opened my eyes—I must have kept them shut during the worst of it—I saw something bloody and slimy lying between my legs, and the goats were eagerly licking it clean with their long, pink tongues. They licked me assiduously, too, to devour all the blood they could come at; clearly it was not for my sake they did it, to clean me after my delivery, but out of desire for the blood itself, as if it were of especial value to them. I had to fend them off as well as I could with what strength remained to me—to hit out at them, at their moist noses.

As soon as I was able I took up the baby and found it was a boy. I tried to tear the navel cord, and finding I could not I bit it in two and took the child in my arms to keep it from the goats. It was now perfectly clean but they would not leave it alone; I had to push them and chase them off continually.

Their behavior was incomprehensible to me and I disliked it. It seemed to me as strange as it was revolting. I staggered up on to my unsteady feet to get out of the place. It was ungrateful of me perhaps, but I couldn't help it; the cave with its acrid stench of goat and its odor of birth nauseated me, and I felt I had to get out of it to breathe. The storm had ceased, so there was no reason to stay, if only my strength sufficed to carry me out. With my newborn babe at my breast I reeled over to the entrance and out into the air, which was fresh after the rain; I had been on the point of fainting but the freshness revived me.

Such was my deliverance, for which I had so greatly longed. That is how it was.

Here the old woman broke off her story. She straightened herself, then bent forward and fiercely poked the fire, which she had been feeding from time to time with a bit of knotty wood.

"And what was it I had brought forth?" she went on fiercely. "That creature sitting over there! That was the fruit of all my love—of the highest human happiness—of all our love for each other, which began by a holy spring; such was its end! Our summer love in the flowering field of corn, witnessed by eagles.

"That was his and my child.

"I could not make it out. It was past understanding. As the child grew and revealed itself I pondered more and more but always in vain upon this baffling question: how could our love have borne such fruit? It is true that when the child was begotten our love was no longer as happy as it had been. Yes, at that time the begetter no longer loved. Was this the reason? Was it this that drew such punishment with it? So dire a punishment?

"But he had loved; why was the child not conceived then? If we were destined to have a child, why did we not have it then, in the high noon of our love? Why did I not conceive until the very last, when my beloved no longer really loved me, when he embraced me without real desire, so that his life sap could not have its proper force? Why was it so? Why did my poor womb not become fruitful until then?

"Was it not strange that I had not conceived long before?

"Perhaps it hadn't happened until the last time we were together—that last, heavy-hearted time which brought joy to neither of us.

"The last time . . . It must have been then, for otherwise far too long a time would have passed before the birth. Even as it was, the period was too long. . . .

"No, I wouldn't think of that! Not of that!

"Often the birth came late. Or at least sometimes. And one never knows quite how to reckon—so many people say that—no, there was no sense at all in trying to explain it. I didn't want to think about it. Not at all. And anyway there was nothing to be gained by it. So one might as well leave it alone. . . . Let one's thoughts work on something else, no matter what. But not on anything so pointless and unrewarding . . .

"I talked like this to myself, persuading myself . . .

"What I did not want to think of was that by women's reckoning the time tallied perfectly with the day my beloved was found dead in the river—the day I was raped by god. And it was soon after that, for the first time in my life, that my monthly flow failed to appear. And at the time of his death it had been long since my beloved lay with me.

"But, I thought, what am I saying? This is madness. And it's impossible—even more impossible . . .

"Begotten by god? God's son—an idiot who is not even a man. A child which if it lives will be a poor idiot without understanding, not even knowing that he is alive; an idiot with a meaningless smirk and a mind like a newborn baby's.

"What an idea! That I could even think of such a thing!

"That I could suppose for a moment that that horrible, monstrous thing in the oracle pit, so savage and inhuman and revolting, had given life to the child—given me a child. Not my love, my great, living, earthly love, but this repulsive thing that I could not recall without the deepest loathing.

"But of course it was quite impossible. A mad notion. Strange that such a notion could occur to me . . .

"And it was not so terribly long since I had been with my beloved—my so deeply beloved—for the last time. He could be the child's father—this child's. Of course he could. If one wished.

"Did I wish it? Did I wish . . .

"No, I couldn't bear to think about it. It drove me to despair—despair of life, love, god, everything.

"God is merciless. Those who say he is good do not know him. He is the most inhuman thing there is. He is wild and incalculable as lightning. Like lightning out of a cloud which one did not know contained lightning. Suddenly it strikes, suddenly he strikes down on one, revealing all his cruelty. Or his love—his cruel love. With him anything may happen. He reveals himself at any time and in anything. The thunderstorm that drove me into the cave, the goats that were sent to take care of me, the scorching summer, charged with unparalleled heat, the birth in the goat cave while heaven hurled its lightnings at the earth, the queer behavior of the goats, their eager interest in the birth and the baby, the vile, repugnant, inhuman events in the goat cave—what lay hidden behind all that? Something divine? Something cruelly, savagely divine? Was there a mighty deity behind it?

"The divine is not human; it is something quite different. And it is not noble or sublime or spiritualized, as one likes to believe. It is alien and repellent and sometimes it is madness. It is malignant and dangerous and fatal. Or so I have found it. And I well know the stench of it—the sour goat-stench—who should know it better than I? It was the first thing I recognized when I entered the cave. The cave in which perhaps I bore a son to a god, a son begotten by the goat-god down there in the holy of holies, in his pit beneath the glorious temple which is consecrated to him as the god of radiance and light—the temple in which I was never permitted to serve him. But I was permitted to bring into the world his witless son, when for some reason he was to be born; an ever leering idiot whom I have had upon my hands all my life. . . .

"No, no. What am I saying? I know nothing, nothing at all about it. . . . I don't know who is father to this child. I didn't know then and I don't know now. God's it cannot be, and it cannot be my beloved's; it bears no likeness to him nor to me—nor to anyone; he is like no human being, and still less like a god. I know nothing.

"But I shake my fist at him who treated me so, who used me in this way, in his pit, his oracle pit— used me as his passive instrument—raped my body and soul, possessed me with his frightful spirit, his delirium, his so-called inspiration, filled me with his hot breath, his alien fire, and my body with his lusting, fertilizing ray so that I had to bear this witless son, who is a mockery of man—of reason and of man —a mockery of me who had to bear him. Who chose me to be his sacrifice, to be possessed by him, to foam at the mouth for god and to bring forth an idiot. Who has exploited me all my life; who stole from me all true happiness, all human happiness; who bereft me of all that others may enjoy—all that gives them security and peace. Who took from me my love, my beloved; all, all—and gave me nothing in return, nothing but himself. Himself. Who is in me still, filling me with his presence, his unrest, never giving me peace because he himself is not peace; never forsaking me. Never forsaking me!

"I shake my fist at him—my impotent fist!"

She trembled, seemingly in a violent tumult of mind. She stirred the fire, and finding that it had gone out tossed the half-charred branch into the smoking embers.

Yet soon she grew a little calmer and controlled herself. And when presently she continued, her voice had regained its natural tone.

"I don't know why I'm telling you all this—you, a stranger. But who is not a stranger to this house?

"You asked me something, and when I began to remember, my life—my whole destiny rose up before me and I was filled with what I remembered. And when did I last speak to anyone? When? It's so long ago that I cannot say.

"I have sat here alone brooding over my fate. There has been time enough for that—too much. But never anyone to tell.

"Yes, my life since I left the world of men—and I never really belonged to it—has been loneliness. I have lived alone here with this child, this son, with this gray-haired man, not knowing even now who he is or whence he came. We have lived alone together up here in the mountains, in this ruinous hovel which I set in order for us I know not how long ago. Our only company has been the goats, which stay by us; wild goats which have always sought us out wherever we have dwelled and which help us to sustain life. They are the only creatures he knows and cares for. But he has always been attracted to the goats and they to him; they follow him wherever he goes and rub against him; one can hardly part them.

"I think of this when I wonder who he is. And I reflect that his face is unstirred by all that people call life—that it has remained the face of a child—a gray-haired child now—with the same unchanging childish smile. The vacant smile that has so tormented and tortured me, and made me feel that I'm living here with an idiot. But sometimes I've wondered whether perhaps it is a god sitting here beside me with his perpetual smile; sitting here looking down at his temple, his Delphi and the whole world of men—just smiling at it all.

"I don't know. I know nothing. But sometimes I

have thought so. Sometimes this idea, too, has crossed my mind."

She ceased and for a time sat silent. Then she rose and went toward the entrance, out toward the night, where a faint light was appearing.

Suddenly she stopped and uttered a cry.

"He's not here! He's not here!"

It was true. He was no longer there. He had vanished.

At some moment during her long story he must have vanished into the night. It was easy to do unobserved, dark as it was in there, and the doorway had no door.

She became quite frantic. Her face could not be discerned, but from her voice the man knew how distraught it must be.

"Where is he? Where is he?" she cried. "Where can he have gone?

"Why has he gone out into the night, into the darkness where he can't look after himself—he'll be killed! He'll fall over the cliff! Why has he done this? Why? Why? Why has he left me?

"Suppose—suppose he understood the bad things I said about him—the horrible things I . . . Suppose he understood! But it's not possible. . . . He's never shown any sign of understanding human speech and never been able to say anything in it. But—perhaps it was just that he never wanted to? Never wanted to have anything to do with such creatures as men are. Sometimes I've almost—yes, sometimes I've wondered whether perhaps he did understand what I said to him in anger, when I was hasty and unreasonable with him—my poor child—my child. Ah, I was, many times, and I was unjust, unjust. . . . How could I . . . How could I say such things—hurt him so—so that he had to leave me. Leave me!"

She was talking to herself, not to the stranger, although she turned to him eagerly meanwhile.

"He must have understood, and that's why . . . Ah, what have I done, what have I done!

"We must go out and search for him," she exclaimed suddenly, despairingly, and stooping she passed through the low entrance and disappeared.

He followed her.

It was a moonlight night and bright with stars, but a light mist of cold lay over the mountains and one could not see far.

She glanced quickly around to make sure that her son was nowhere near the house, and then set off at once along a track—it might have been a track, though it was difficult to distinguish—leading uphill into the mountains. She walked so swiftly that he could hardly keep up, being unaccustomed to such terrain. It seemed incredible that one of her age could move so rapidly. But she had lived the greater part of her life in these hills and was one with them. With her old feet swathed in almost worn-out goatskin she glided along the mountain side almost without effort as if she belonged to it, like a gray animal, almost impossible to make out in the misty moon-light. She walked like the wild animals of the region. He followed her, marveling at what she had told him of herself and of this son whom they were seeking up here among the mists. God's son?

It was certainly an animal track that they were fol-lowing, and not one used by men. Theirs ran some-where lower down, though it was hidden by the haze. Why she chose this particular path he did not know, but supposed that for some reason she believed her son must have passed this way. She could be sure he had not gone down toward Delphi, for he could never have been there in his life. Had she spied some foot-print? Perhaps, since she took this way so deter-minedly.

It was a gentle climb at first, but later it became very steep. They came right in among the hills, and the path—invisible to him—sloped ever more sharply upward. But once they had reached more level ground—perhaps a plateau—she halted. The invisible track must fork here, or she must have lost the trail, for she stopped and hesitated, gazing out over the bare mountain landscape. The moonlight filtered through the thin cold mist and made everything look strange; it seemed to him that one might have doubts about anything and everything in this half-real world. But soon she went on again and now seemed certain of her way. He had the queer impression that although she was a woman she moved instinctively like the beasts, or was perhaps guided by some other sense not possessed by ordinary mortals. They continued further and further into unreality. The ground began rising again.

All at once the mist lifted and in the sharp moonlight they saw before them a mighty peak covered with everlasting snow, white and dark and mysterious under the sparkling stars. A slow climb led them up to the edge of the snow, into which a narrow but distinct track wound and disappeared. Whither it led one could not tell; it merely ceased, vanished. It was odd, the way this path vanished beneath the eternal snows. The old woman began to make her way along it.

After a little while she stooped and picked up something from the ground. It was a goatskin girdle. She examined it eagerly and then lowered the hand that held it, drawing a deep breath. She went on. Soon afterwards she found a kilt, also of goatskin, discarded beside the path. This, too, she picked up and laid over her arm without a word. Further up she found a sandal and not long afterwards another, simply made from a piece of hide and a thong. It lay quite near the edge of the snow. They stopped there and looked up at the mysterious mountain.

A thin layer of fresh snow had fallen during the night, and on it they saw the clear print of a naked foot in a line with the path. As they continued up-

ward they found one footprint after another—someone had walked barefoot up toward the eternal
snows. They were the light, distinct tracks of quite a
small, delicate foot, becoming fainter and fainter until at last they were no more than a hint, an almost
imperceptible touch upon the snow. Then they
ceased altogether. No trail led back.

The old woman stood and looked at these vanish-
ing traces of a foot that had ceased to touch the
ground—of a being who had lost all weight and had
risen into space, which here on the mountain of god
was so clear that it seemed one could touch its stars.

"He has gone back," she murmured softly to herself. "It is as I thought.

"He used to come up here, when he did leave our
hut," she added. "It was this place that drew him.
Now he has thrown off the garments in which he
hid, his earthly husk, and become again what he really
was. The father has fetched him home . . ."

She was silent, and what stirred in her, what she
really thought and felt, she did not betray. Over her
arm she carried the things from which he had freed
himself—the things she had given him, fashioned
with her own hands; and perhaps she felt a stab at
her human mother-heart because he had done this—
thrown them away; but if so she did not show it. In
her furrowed old face nothing was to be deciphered,
and nothing seen of the ferment she had shown before, now that she understood what had happened;

understood it all. Yet it is likely that much of her long life passed before her mind's eye in this hour, when all things seemed to have reached their end and the dark riddle had found its solution, its explanation, in the tracks across the eternal snows. For a moment she kept her eyes shut as she seemed always to do, the stranger recalled from her story, when her innermost self was filled with some power. Then she opened them again, these ancient eyes which seemed to have seen all things. And yet again she looked down at the signs of his departure—at the light imprints of a foot that was unusually small and delicate for a full-grown man.

"He had such beautiful feet," she said, as if reproaching herself for not having given proper thought to this. "His hands and feet were so beautiful."

She lingered there for a little; then began slowly walking down across the blanket of snow toward the gray ground, to the earth. She began the homeward way.

She walked more slowly now, though the path ran downhill, and she was no longer in any hurry. Perhaps she was deep in thought and that was why she moved more slowly than before. If so she may well have been thinking of the son whose slight earthly possessions she was now carrying back to her hut and her solitude. And perhaps also of the mighty father who had begotten him upon her.

The stranger following her was also thinking of

this son who had ascended from the strange mountain, having cast off his goatskin garments, the disguise that he had worn as the son of a god who was evidently a goat-god, too, though surely more than that. He wondered whether it had been a gray-haired man who rose up from the snow with that last hovering step, into starry space; or whether by then he had regained eternal youth. No doubt he had, and his face was different even then; more like a god's.

He reflected that the son of god who was the source of his own appalling fate—who had flung the frightful curse upon him—was said to have ascended into heaven from a mountain, too, and was received by the father-god in a cloud, if one were to believe those who worshipped and loved him. But he had first been crucified, which according to them made him extraordinary and his life full of every sort of meaning and significance, for every age. Whereas this son of god seemed to have been born merely to sit at the dim entrance of a ruinous goat hut and look out over the world and the breed of men and their many inventions, and his own magnificent temple, and laugh at it all.

Suddenly he knew of what that perpetual smile reminded him. It was the image of a god which he had seen yesterday, down in the temple at Delphi: an ancient image standing somewhat apart as if to make room for newer, finer images. It had the same smile, enigmatic and remote, at once meaningless and inscrutable. A smile neither good nor evil, yet for that very reason frightening. It represented the same god as did the other images, no doubt—her god and the temple's—but it was evidently very old, and so was the riddle of its stone smile.

Yes, god was incomprehensible, cruel and frightening. She, too, had found him so—this sibyl who had known him as no one else had known him, who had been possessed by him, loved and cursed by him, who had lived her whole life for him and had even borne him a son. A son who must have come into the world just to show that meaninglessness, too, is divine. Or to be revenged upon her because she loved the one-armed man—because she rested one summer upon his single arm. Because she had experienced something other than god. Another love than the love of god.

Yes, god is evil. She was right in that. Heartless and malignant. Revengeful toward anyone who dares to love another than him. Toward him who dares forbid him to lean his head against his house. Cruel and merciless. He cares nothing for mankind, only for himself. And he never forgives, never forgets.

But neither do I care for anyone but myself. And I hate him as he hates me. If he has cursed me, then I curse him, too.

I will not bow. And I am immortal as he is! He himself made me so—though from malice and not for my enjoyment. It is a part of his curse, the cruelest part of it. I am immortal! Though my immortality is not like his.

He reigns in the highest; he is ascended into eternal youth in his heaven, after hanging on a cross for a few hours, while I must be tormented forever here on earth. I must wander here, unblessed in my soul, pursued by the unrest with which he has filled me and never finding peace. Doomed to live on in this world, which he left long ago, and to possess no other. And to look about me day after day, year after year, for centuries and tens of centuries, with these old eyes that see through everything and perceive the vanity of all things. In a world covered with ashes. It is for this that he has chosen me, condemned me. But I will not bow. And my hatred is as immortal as his!

Thus he reflected, distraught by his destiny, as he followed the old woman's gray figure moving on ahead.

They had to cover the last part of the way by the light of the stars alone, but it was this part that she knew best. The mist had gone. When they reached the hut the first dawnlight of the new day was appearing, and they sat down on the clumsy stone bench outside; they did not go in. There was no sunshine anywhere in that landscape, but a faint brightness showed that it would come.

He was still in his stormy mood, and suddenly he

broke out heatedly as if he were in the middle of a fierce dispute with her: "How you must hate this god who has treated you so, and done these things to you! How you must hate a being so full of insensate evil as he is!"

The old woman did not answer at once, and seemed to be reflecting. Then she said, "I don't know who he is. How then can I hate him? Or love him? I believe I neither hate him nor love him.

"When I think about it, it seems to me that such words have no meaning when applied to him. He is not as we are and we can never understand him. He is incomprehensible, inscrutable. He is god.

"And so far as I comprehend it he is both evil and good, both light and darkness, both meaningless and full of a meaning which we can never perceive, yet never cease to puzzle over. A riddle which is intended not to be solved but to exist. To exist for us always. To trouble us always.

"The most incomprehensible thing about him is that he can also be a little turf altar where we may lay a few ears of corn and so be at ease and at peace. He may be a spring where we can mirror our faces and drink sweet, fresh water from our hands. He can be that, too, I know. Though he was not that for me —I think he could not be.

"For me he has been a wild chasm which engulfed me and all that I held dear. A glowing breath and an embrace without safety, without peace, but for which I longed nevertheless. A hot and alien power which ruled my ways.

"He has made me very unhappy. But he has also allowed me to know a happiness passing all understanding. He has, and I must not forget it.

"What would my life have been without him? If I had never been filled with him, with his spirit? If I had never felt the bliss that poured from him, the anguish and pain that is his also, and the wonder of being annihilated in his blazing arms, of being altogether his? Of feeling his rapture, his boundless bliss, and sharing god's infinite happiness in being alive?

"What would I have been without that? If I had never experienced anything but myself?

"Yet I cannot forget all the evil he has done me, and the horror. How he took possession of my whole life and took from me almost every earthly joy. How he opened his abysses to me, his evil depths. I don't forget that, and I don't forgive!

"But sitting here, old and alone, looking back— looking back over my life, it is you, my god, that I think of. For it is you who have been my life, you who consume and burn all things like fire. You who leave nothing in your wake. My life is what I have lived in you. The cruel, bitter, rich life you have given me. May you be cursed and blessed!"

He looked at her in silence; at her dark face, which

seemed ravaged by fire, and at her inscrutable old eyes which had seen god.

His eyes too had seen god. But because of that they were empty, like dried-up wells, like depths with nothing in them. They were not like hers. Why was that? Why was he so poor and she so rich?

"But my fate. What have you to say of that?" he demanded fiercely. "What have you to tell me—me, the man who comes to you seeking an interpretation of this tumult in his soul, of the curse that lies on him? What comfort have you for me? The things that bring you comfort and meaning hold nothing for me."

The old woman looked at him and met his gaze. It was poor, indeed—it was the poorest look she had seen in anyone. She had noticed it when he came, and noticed that his simple mantle was like a king's robe in comparison.

But she saw, too, that he was wrong in what he said: that his eyes were dried-up wells, depths with nothing in them. It was not so. They were not empty. They were full of despair. If the curse that had fallen upon him had made him destitute and taken everything from him, it had at least brought him this. And perhaps because she saw this, she answered as she did.

"I can see in your face that you're under god's curse and that what you say is true. It's plain that you're not free, that you're bound to him and that he doesn't mean to let you go. He is your destiny. Your soul is filled with him; through his curse you live a life with god. You hate him, you mock and revile him. But judging by your indignant words you care for nothing in the world but him, and are filled with him alone. With what you call your hatred of him. But this very red-hot hatred of god is perhaps your experience of the divine.

"Perhaps one day he will bless you instead of cursing you. I don't know. Perhaps one day you will let him lean his head against your house. Perhaps you won't. I know nothing about that. But whatever you may do, your fate will be forever bound up with god, your soul forever filled with god.

"You want me to look into the future. I can't do that. But I know enough of the life of mankind and can glimpse enough of the road that lies before them to know that they can never escape the curse and the blessing that comes to them from god. Whatever they may think and do, whatever they may believe or disbelieve, their destiny will always be bound up with god."

She ceased and turned from him. She looked away, he knew not where. Perhaps toward the distant mountains which already lay in sunlight, though they themselves remained in deep shadow. Perhaps over no earthly landscape, but over one opening before her inner vision. At any rate she seemed far away from him; it was as if she were no longer aware of his presence.

But he sat looking at her, filled with her words. They seemed to interpret his destiny in another way; they allowed him to see into it, to glimpse something there which he had never thought of and which perhaps would make it even less endurable. It no longer seemed quite as meaningless and hopeless as before. Perhaps not even as unchanging as he had thought. But that was something to which his endless wandering must give the answer—the endless road that lay before him. For it was as she had said: I know nothing about that.

They sat silent for a long time.

At last he rose. He must continue his journey; he must set forth again. When he took his leave she moved her head slightly but said nothing. They parted in silence, without words. He went down the steep slope toward Delphi, and she stayed behind, watching him go and looking out over the ancient valley, with its city and its temple and all the things she knew so well. The sunshine had come down there now; people were busy outside their houses, and coming and going in the streets. The temple court still lay empty, but a youth was sweeping the ground before the entrance to the temple. Then he garnished it with fresh laurels from the god's grove. Up the sacred way a young woman was walking slowly toward the holy place, dressed as a bride and attended by reverent people, and perhaps also by people not so reverent. Her eyes were lifted up toward the holy place, and surely her face was full of the rapture she was soon to feel, and perhaps also of fear of what lay before her. The morning sun poured down upon the crowd as it moved forward—down over the whole valley and the mountains around it—down on all that mighty landscape.

She sat looking out over it all with her old eyes.

Pär Lagerkvist (1891-1974) was the author of more than thirty-five books and was renowned for his versatility as a poet, dramatist, essayist and novelist. In 1940 he was elected one of the eighteen "Immortals" of the Swedish Academy, and in 1951 he was awarded the Nobel Prize for Literature. Another of his works, *Barabbas*, is also available in Vintage.

Dedications:

JOHN: To Eric Stephenson and Robert Kirkman for helping get the ball rolling. And Drew Gill for his help keeping it moving every month and every issue.

ROB: For Thomas and Harold.

Thanks:

Taylor Wells, for the coloring assists.
Tom B. Long, for the logo.
Comicbookfonts.com, for the fonts.

And More Thanks:

Rich Amtower, Jeff Branget, David Brothers, Ryan "Pimp Slap" Browne, Fiona Staples, Maricio Malacay, Skybound, Joshie Williamson, and Brian K. Vaughan.

Olive's wardrobe courtesy of Ryan Browne and Josh Willamson & Skybound and Brian K. Vaughan & Fiona Staples. God Hates Astronauts, Ghosted and Saga images copyright their respective owners.

Chapter 1

 PART 4 ½ OF 5

written & lettered by
John Layman

drawn & coloured by
Rob Guillory

Color Assists: Taylor Wells

Fonts: Comicraft (comicbookfonts.com)
Logo: Tombgraphics (tombgraphics.com)
Book Design: Rob Guillory & John Layman

www.ChewComic.com

KNOCK
KNOCK
KNOCK

SAGE?

HI, TONI.

SAGE!

OH MY GOSH! BABY SISTER! IT'S SO GOOD TO SEE YOU!

WHAT ARE YOU *DOING* HERE?

I GOT MYSELF INTO TROUBLE, TONI.

I NEED *HELP.*

SAGE AND ANTONELLE CHU ARE SISTERS.

AND, LIKE OTHER SIBLINGS IN THEIR FAMILY, EACH HAS THEIR OWN EXTRAORDINARY ABILITY BASED ON MATERIAL THEY CONSUME.

TONI IS *CIBOVOYANT*.

ABLE TO FLASH ONTO THE *FUTURE* OF ANY LIVING BEING SHE INGESTS.

SAGE IS *CIPROPANTHROPATIC*.

ABLE TO SEE THE MEMORIES OF ANYONE NEARBY EATING THE SAME THING.

FURRIES GO HARD.

TONI HAS HAS LESS THAN A WEEK TO LIVE.

AND SHE *KNOWS* IT.

SNAP

SAGE HAS RECENTLY MADE AN ENEMY OF DON FEDERICO BISCOTTI--

MURDERER!!!

--WHO INTENDS FOR SAGE TO BE DEAD AS SOON AS POSSIBLE AS WELL.

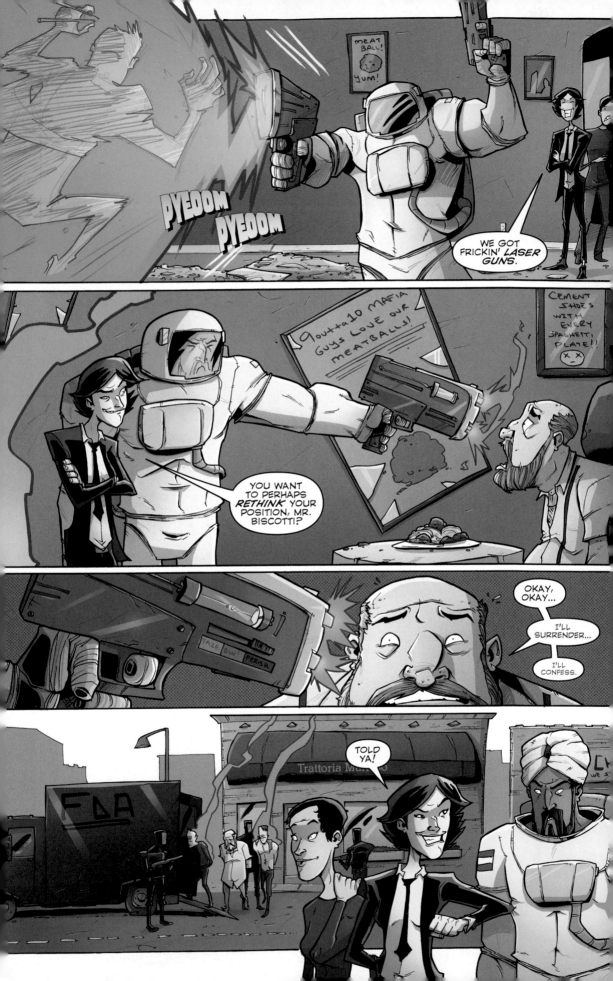

END SPACE
CAKES:
CHAPTER IV½.

ALSO: END
FAMILY
RECIPES:
CHAPTER I.

Chapter 2

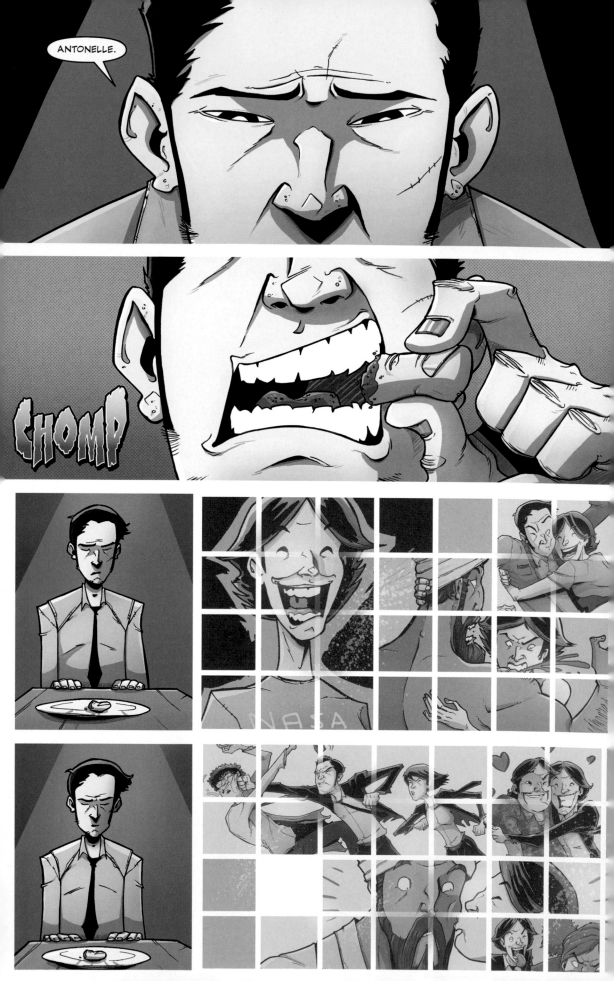

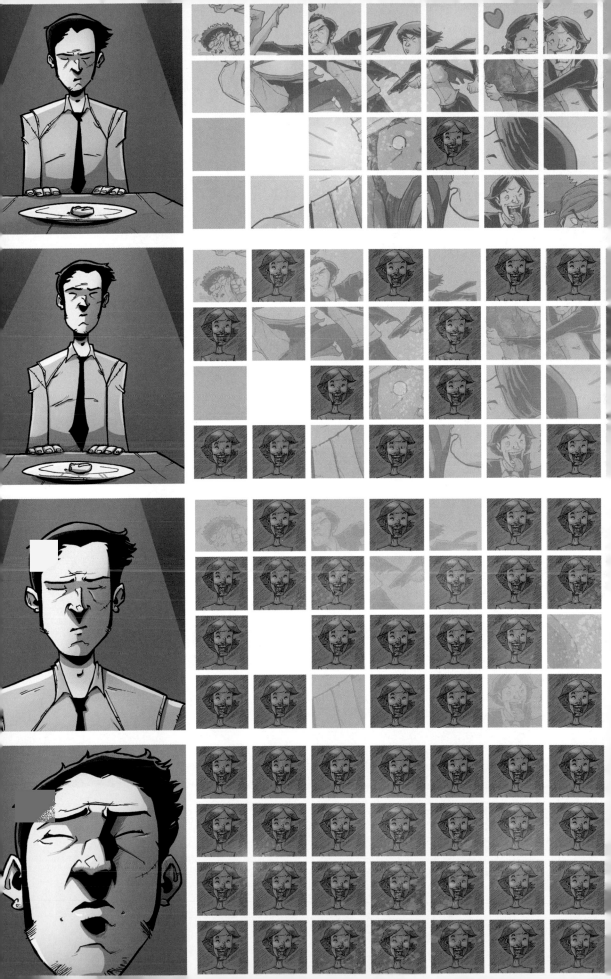

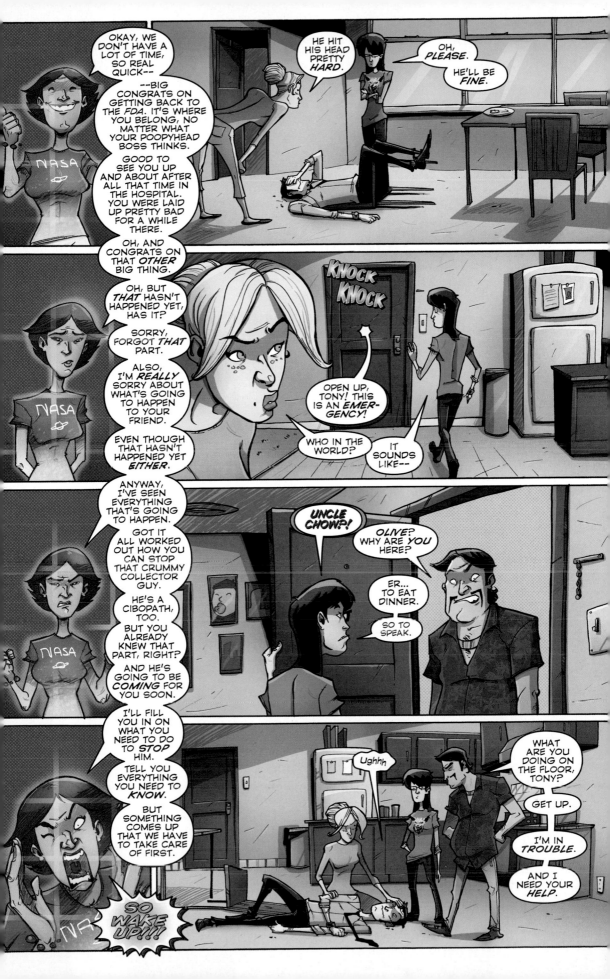

KEN KEEBLER IS AN EROSCIBOPICTAROS.

ABLE TO TAKE PICTURES OF FOOD THAT INSPIRE EROTIC FEELINGS IN THE VIEWER, LONGING, AND SEXUAL DESIRE.

HE'S A *FOOD PORNO-GRAPHER.*

EARLY IN HIS CAREER KEEBLER TRIED HIS HAND AT *OTHER* TYPES OF PHOTOGRAPHY--

--BUT DISCOVERED QUICKLY HIS SNAPSHOTS OF *CUISINE* HAD A STRANGE AND UNSETTLING EFFECT ON PEOPLE.

AND ALL THEIR BASE, PUERILE, *FILTHY* INTERESTS.

COOKBOOKS 'n more!!!

ADULTS ONLY!

AND THAT THERE WAS *GOOD MONEY* TO BE MADE BY SERVING A MORE *SPECIALIZED* NICHE OF CULINARY ENTHUSIASTS.

END *FAMILY RECIPES: CHAPTER II.*

Chapter 3

END PROLOGUE.

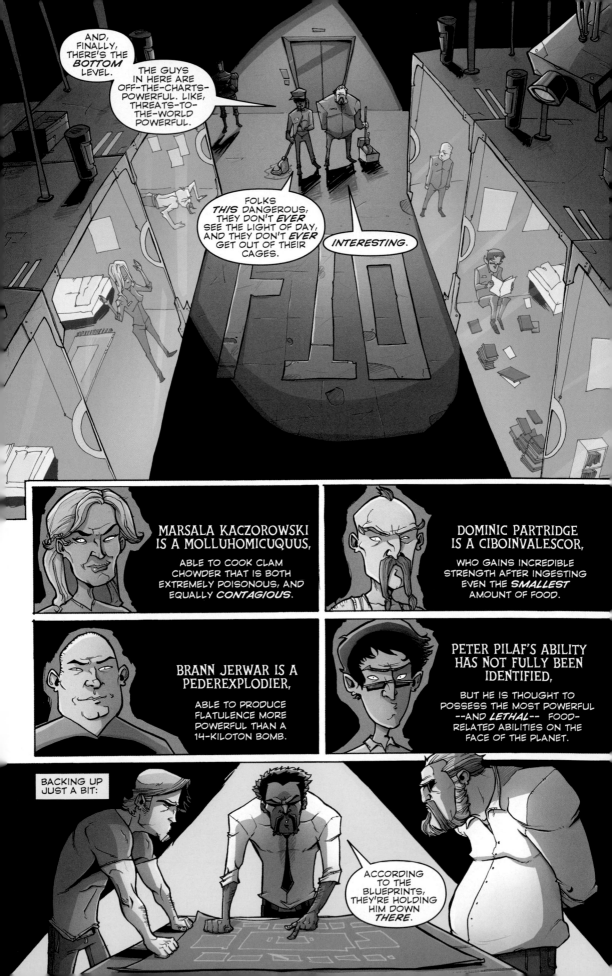

AND, FINALLY, THERE'S THE *BOTTOM* LEVEL. THE GUYS IN HERE ARE OFF-THE-CHARTS-POWERFUL. LIKE, THREATS-TO-THE-WORLD POWERFUL.

FOLKS *THIS* DANGEROUS, THEY DON'T *EVER* SEE THE LIGHT OF DAY, AND THEY DON'T *EVER* GET OUT OF THEIR CAGES.

INTERESTING.

MARSALA KACZOROWSKI IS A MOLLUHOMICUQUUS,

ABLE TO COOK CLAM CHOWDER THAT IS BOTH EXTREMELY POISONOUS, AND EQUALLY *CONTAGIOUS*.

DOMINIC PARTRIDGE IS A CIBOINVALESCOR,

WHO GAINS INCREDIBLE STRENGTH AFTER INGESTING EVEN THE *SMALLEST* AMOUNT OF FOOD.

BRANN JERWAR IS A PEDEREXPLODIER,

ABLE TO PRODUCE FLATULENCE MORE POWERFUL THAN A 14-KILOTON BOMB.

PETER PILAF'S ABILITY HAS NOT FULLY BEEN IDENTIFIED,

BUT HE IS THOUGHT TO POSSESS THE MOST POWERFUL --AND *LETHAL*-- FOOD-RELATED ABILITIES ON THE FACE OF THE PLANET.

BACKING UP JUST A BIT:

ACCORDING TO THE BLUEPRINTS, THEY'RE HOLDING HIM DOWN *THERE*.

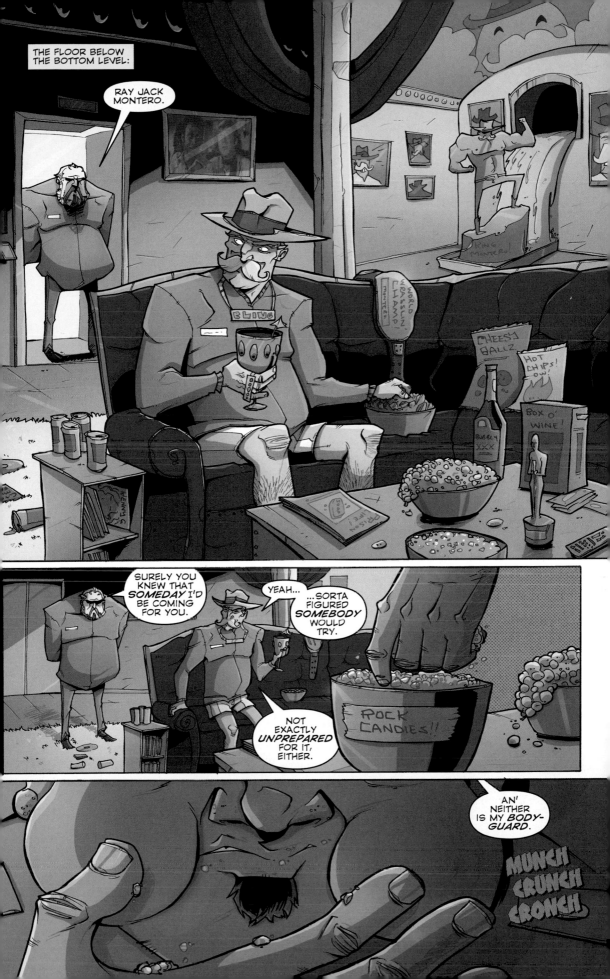

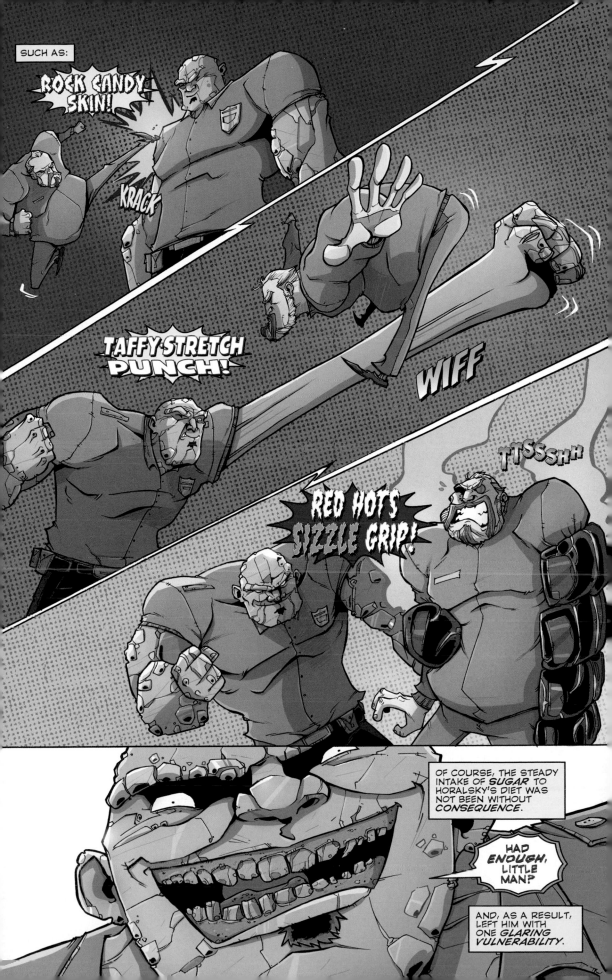

END *FAMILY RECIPES*: CHAPTER *III*.

Chapter 4

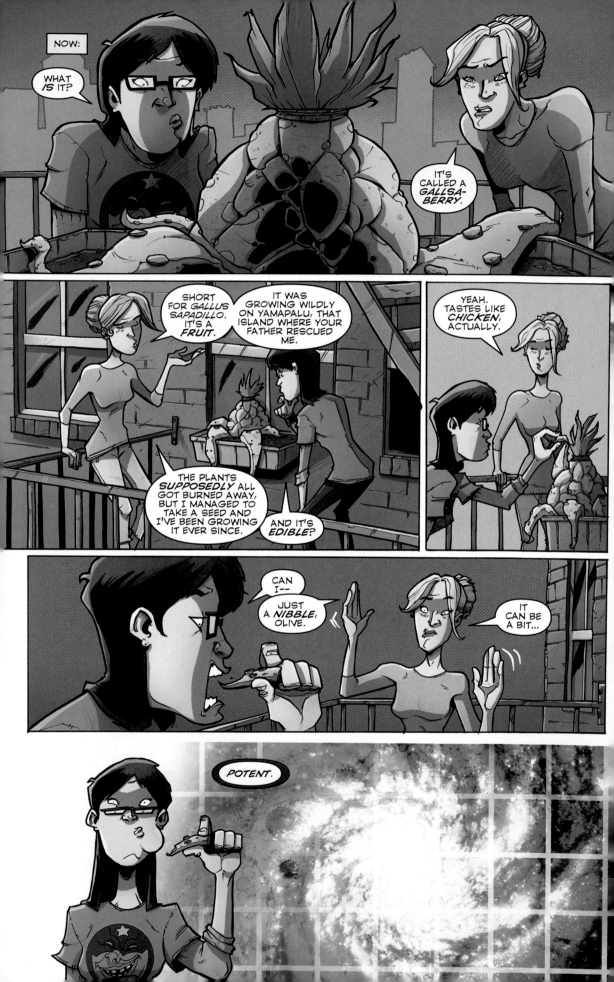

JUST A BIT LATER:

YOU *SURE* HE'S NOT GOING TO NOTICE?

POSITIVE. AND EVEN IF HE *DOES*, HE'S NOT GOING TO CARE.

HI, TONY.

OH, HEY, DAD.

<grunt>

YOU *OKAY*, TONY?

Mm.

BYE, TONY!

BYE, DAD!

<grunt>

YOU *GOT* IT?

YEAH, I GOT IT. THIS IS SO COOL.

OLIVE CHU IS A CIBOPATH, LIKE HER FATHER.

SHE IS ALSO FAR, *FAR* MORE POWERFUL THAN HER FATHER, ABLE TO SHUT OFF HER POWER WHENEVER SHE DESIRES.

AND *ABSORB* MEMORIES AND ABILITIES OF THOSE SHE CONSUMES WITH FAR GREATER SPEED AND EFFICIENCY.

HERSHEL BROWN WAS AN XOCOSCALPERE

ABLE TO SCULPT *CHOCOLATE* WITH SUCH ACCURACY AND VERISIMILITUDE THAT ANYTHING HE CRAFTED COULD *EXACTLY* MIMIC ITS REAL-LIFE COUNTERPART.

AFTER BROWN MET AN UNFORTUNATE END, A BIT OF *HIM* CAME INTO OLIVE'S POSSESSION.

OLIVE NOW POSSESSES *MORE* THAN A BIT OF HIS XOCOSCALPERE ABILITY.

FDA: CALORIES? WHAT ARE CALORIES?

Scrip Scrape Scrip

WHILE ALSO INHERITING *ALL* OF HER FATHER'S TEMPER.

HEY, FUCKERS.

Chapter 5

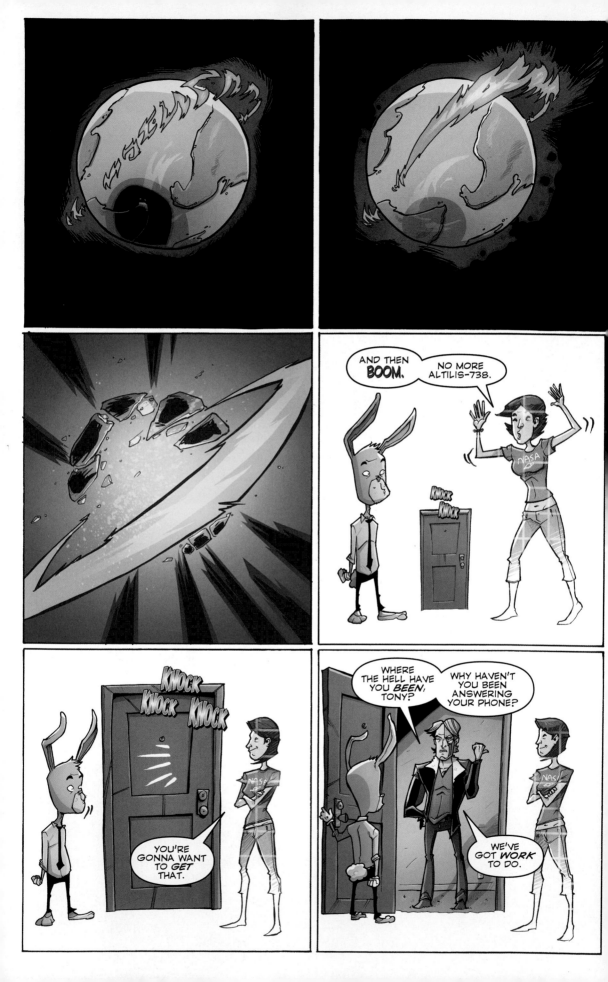

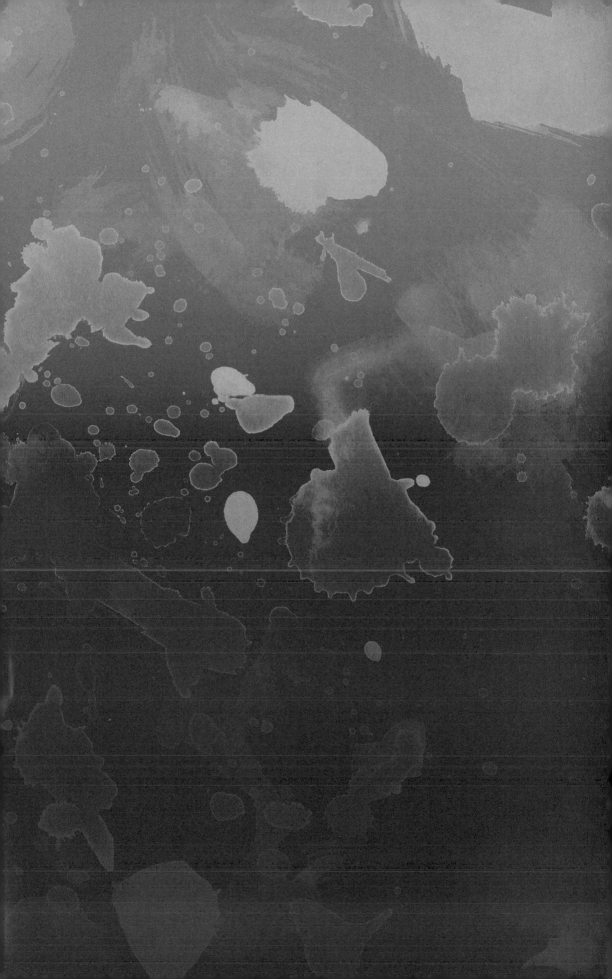

CHEW #37 Covers A +B.

CHEW #37 Covers + CHEW #39 Cover.

ABOVE: The greatest commission EVER.

JOHN LAYMAN

A Karate black-belt, billionaire philanthropist and People magazine's two-time back-to-back Sexiest Man Alive winner, CHEW writer and co-creator John Layman enjoys deep-sea shark-wrestling, extreme motocross, nude volcano surfing, amateur tracheotomies and slight embellishments to his biography.

ROB GUILLORY

Rob Guillory was raised by wolves in the mean, MEAN swamps of Lafayette, Louisiana. At age 5, he killed his first alligator with a boomerang made of rage. Now at age 31, he fights giant nutria in his backyard with the assistance of his very pregnant wife and his three-year-old son. He has several hats, under which he hides many knives.

ChewComic.com

For Original Art Sales, please visit RobGuilloryStore.com.